Book
Sale

Pete Crenshaw was acting as lookout while his ~~~
Jupiter and Bob snuck into the P~~ ~~~. A low
stone tower. ~~~ent signal. Pete bent to the

Pete's ~~~

"Jupe? Bob?"

Jupiter's voice came very low. "Someone is in
the tower, and he's after us! The only place we
could go was up! We're on the second floor—"

There was a sudden silence. Then, "He's coming
up! We've got to go higher!"

The walkie-talkie went dead.

The Mystery
of the
Purple Pirate

by
William Arden

based on characters created by Robert Arthur

BULLSEYE BOOKS
ALFRED A. KNOPF • NEW YORK

Contents

A Challenge from Hector Sebastian

Hello, mystery lovers! Once again it's my pleasure to introduce an action-packed case of the Three Investigators. First let me introduce the young super-sleuths. There's Jupiter Jones, First Investigator, a chunky boy fond of a good meal and a good puzzle. His razor-sharp memory and brilliant powers of deduction have gotten the team out of a number of tight corners. Then there's the tall and athletic Second Investigator, Peter Crenshaw, nervous in the face of danger but bold in meeting it head on. The last but not least is Bob Andrews, in charge of Records and Research—a reliable and quiet young man, indispensable to his fellow Investigators.

This time the junior detectives take on a mind-teasing case at the Purple Pirate Lair and aboard the pirate ship *Black Vulture*. Certain strange events lead them to believe one pirate is still very much alive at the former haven of California's notorious privateers.

The mysterious adventure tests the boys' insight and repeatedly gets them into tight corners. Match wits with the Three Investigators and see if you can beat them to the solution of *The Mystery of the Purple Pirate*!

HECTOR SEBASTIAN

The Mystery
of the
Purple Pirate

1
Buccaneers, Brigands, and Bandits!

When his alarm clock rang violently, Pete Crenshaw opened one eye and groaned. Only the second week of summer vacation and already he wished bitterly that he'd never agreed to do yard work for his next-door neighbors while they were away on a trip. But the funds of the junior detective agency to which he belonged were at an all-time low after an end-of-school trip to Disneyland, and the team needed summer money. The other two sleuths had also been put to work: Bob Andrews had a part-time job at the library, and Jupiter Jones had reluctantly agreed to work extra hours at The Jones Salvage Yard, where he lived with his aunt and uncle.

With a final groan, Pete crawled out of bed and hurried into his clothes. When he dragged himself into the kitchen, he saw that his father was already having breakfast.

"Too early for you, Pete?" Mr. Crenshaw said, grinning.

"Got to do that dumb yard work," Pete grumbled as he got his orange juice from the refrigerator.

"Summer money, eh? Well, maybe there's an easier way. This was left in our mailbox last night."

Mr. Crenshaw put a yellow sheet of paper at Pete's place as the boy sat down. Pete glanced at the paper while he drank his juice. It was one of those advertising flyers that local businesses pay to have delivered house to house. As Pete read his excitement grew:

BUCCANEERS!   BRIGANDS!

Lovers of adventure!   Historians!
Bookworms!   Descendants of pirates!

The Society for Justice to Buccaneers, Brigands, Bandits, and Bushwhackers *will pay $25 an hour to anyone who can report detailed information about local pirates,* *bandits, highwaymen, and other colorful miscreants of California's lusty past.*

Come to 1995 De La Vina Street
any day of the week, June 18–22,
from 9 to 5.

BANDITS!   BUSHWACKERS!

"Wow!" Pete yelled. "We can make a fortune, Dad! I mean, we know a lot about old-time crooks around here, especially Jupiter! I've got to show this to Jupe and Bob right away. Today's the eighteenth, and it's almost eight already!"

"Whoa," Mr. Crenshaw said. "Before you become a millionaire, finish your breakfast."

"Dad! I have to water the lawn, then—"

"You boys always think better on a full stomach, especially Jupiter. Force something down."

Pete groaned. "Just some cereal then!"

He ate the cereal quickly, then sniffed the plate of hotcakes and bacon his father set down in front of him.

"Well," Pete said, "maybe just one plate."

While his Dad grinned but said nothing, Pete finished the hotcakes and bacon, had another plateful, and then picked up the advertising flyer and ran out. He hurried next door, watered the lawn, impatiently raked the fallen leaves and branches, then jumped onto his bike. He pedaled hard, and it was just nine o'clock when he rode up to the long, colorful fence of The Jones Salvage Yard. The fence had been decorated by local artists. Near one corner it showed a ship foundering in a green ocean as a painted fish looked on. Pete pressed the fish's eye and the board swung open—this was Green Gate One.

Pete slipped through and stood in Jupiter's outdoor workshop, located close to the boys' hidden headquarters in an old mobile home trailer. The trailer was the center of operations of The Three Investigators detective agency. Pete was the Second Investigator of the team. Leaving his bike by two others in the workshop, Pete crawled into the mouth of a long corrugated pipe that was too narrow for an adult to enter. The pipe, named Tunnel Two, led under a great mound of junk that totally surrounded the house trailer. By now everyone else had forgotten that the trailer was even in the salvage yard. At the end of the dark pipe, Pete pushed up a trapdoor and emerged into the small trailer room, which was filled with furniture and all the equipment the boys used in their detective work.

"Guys! Look at this!"

Pete waved the yellow flyer. Then he stopped

and stared. Jupiter Jones, the chubby and very brainy First Investigator of the team, was standing near the desk. Bob Andrews, the small, blond, and studious Records and Research man, was leaning against a filing cabinet. Both of them held the same yellow flyer!

Bob sighed. "I got here five minutes ago, Second, with the same big news!"

"Which I already had," Jupiter said. "It appears, fellows, we all had the same idea for making money!"

Pete climbed all the way inside the hidden room and dropped into an overstuffed armchair they had retrieved from the salvage yard.

"I guess we're all tired of work already," Pete decided.

"Work never hurt anyone," Jupiter reproved the Second Investigator and then slumped into the desk chair. "But I must admit that spending day after day in the salvage yard is cruel and inhuman. Perhaps the Society for Justice to Buccaneers, Brigands, Bandits, and Bushwhackers will come to our rescue."

"Anything for a little extra money," Bob said.

"Who should we tell them about?" Pete asked.

"Well, of course there's the French privateer de Bouchard," said Jupe. "He's the most famous pirate in California history."

Pete said, "There's El Diablo, the bandit we learned about in the Moaning Cave case."

"And those soldiers who killed Don Sebastián Alvaro to get the Cortés Sword in the Headless Horse case," Bob added.

"Oh, and that follower of de Bouchard's —William Evans, the Purple Pirate," Jupiter continued. He glanced at the old grandfather clock they had rebuilt. "But we aren't the only ones who know those stories, so I suggest we move swiftly."

Suiting action to words, the trio dropped through the trapdoor and crawled through Tunnel Two to the workshop. As they emerged they heard, "Jupiter! Where have you gotten to? Jupiter!"

"It's your aunt Mathilda, Jupe!" said Bob.

The caller could not be seen over the piles of junk that surrounded the workshop, but her voice came closer and closer.

"I'll bet she's got work for us to do!" exclaimed Pete.

Jupiter turned pale. "Hurry!"

The boys grabbed their bikes, slipped through Green Gate One, and rode off toward downtown Rocky Beach. As they neared the address on De La Vina Street, Bob realized he knew it.

"It's an old Spanish-style courtyard surrounded by a stucco wall, with shops at the far end of the court. Most of them are empty."

Jupiter puffed heavily as he pedaled. "That's probably why the society picked it, Records. They undoubtedly rented it cheaply, and it will be a quiet place for interviews."

As the boys turned into the 1900 block of De La Vina, they saw a small crowd, growing larger by the minute, gathered in front of closed wooden gates in the high wall of number 1995. Jupiter studied the crowd as they rode up.

"A few adults, but mostly teenagers and kids," the stout leader of the team observed. "Because it's a workday, the adults won't come until later. An advantage for us, fellows."

As they locked their bikes to a convenient iron railing, the boys saw the high wooden gates open and a dapper little man with white hair and a big, bushy mustache come out. He wore a tweed jacket, riding breeches, boots, and a silk scarf at his throat, and he carried a riding crop. He looked like some old-time cavalryman. The man faced the crowd and raised his riding crop for silence.

"My name is Major Karnes! I want to welcome all of you to the Society for Justice to Buccaneers, Brigands, Bandits, and Bushwhackers. We will interview all of you, but there are too many of you today, so we will have to limit our interviews to those who came the farthest! Only those who live beyond the city limits of Rocky Beach will be interviewed now; the rest can go home. Do come back another day."

A cry of disappointment went up from the crowd. The teenagers began to push and shove. Backing away, Major Karnes bumped into the high wooden doors, closing them behind him! Backed against the gates, he tried to speak, but the teenagers drowned him out.

"Hey, what's goin' on?"

"You mean we came all this way for nothin'?"

"You've got a lot of nerve!"

Major Karnes swung his riding crop at the rowdy teenagers. "Get away from me, you young punks!"

The crowd turned ugly. A teenager grabbed the small man's riding crop and threw it away. The others surged toward him. Major Karnes went pale.

"Help! Hubert!"

The angry crowd pressed closer!

2

Cheated!

"Help!" Major Karnes cried as the furious teenagers closed in on him. "Hubert! Help!"

Pete turned quickly to Jupiter. "Hey, this is getting out of hand. Get the major inside." With that, the tall, muscular Second Investigator leaped on top of a nearby parked car and pointed up the street.

"Police!" he shouted. "The police are coming!"

The teenagers turned from the gates and looked up at Pete in alarm. Bob and Jupiter quickly slipped through the crowd and reached the major.

"Come on!" Pete yelled. "Let's get out of here!"

He jumped down from the car and ran toward the far end of the street. Some of the teenagers began to run after him at once, while others hesitated. Behind them, Bob pulled the heavy wooden gates open a crack.

"This way, sir," said Jupiter and pushed the major inside. A few moments later Pete appeared from among the dispersing teenagers and slipped into the courtyard after Major Karnes, Jupiter, and Bob. Together the boys pulled the heavy gates shut again as Major Karnes leaned panting against the inner wall.

"*Hubert!*" he bawled. "Young punks! The police should throw them all in prison!"

The courtyard was paved with large stones from long ago, and jacaranda and pepper trees grew from open spaces among them. The high wall, almost hidden by brightly flowered shrubs, extended all around the courtyard, and a short row of shops lined the far end. The shops all looked empty. A lone small truck was parked in front of the stores.

The major took a red bandanna from his jacket pocket and mopped his brow. "Thanks for helping, boys, but I'd have liked to see the police take care of that rabble!"

Pete laughed. "There weren't any police, sir. I had to think of something to get their attention and scare them so they'd forget all about attacking you."

"And give us time to open the gates," Bob added.

The major gaped. "By gad, that was quick thinking. Well, for that you will be the first interviewed no matter where you live! *Hubert, you idiot! Come out here!*"

"Gosh, thank you, sir!" Pete and Bob exclaimed.

"Only fair."

Jupiter frowned. "I'm afraid the crowd outside will think this is preferential treatment."

"I won't be browbeaten by a pack of schoolboys!" the major snapped. "*Hubert, you imbecile! Where are you?!*"

The door of one of the empty shops burst open at last and an enormous, hulking giant came running toward the little major. Looking like an elephant in a gray chauffeur's uniform that was too small, the massive newcomer had a round face that could have been any age. A ridiculous little chauffeur's hat was perched on his thick red hair, and his blue eyes were frightened.

"I-I'm sorry, M-M-Major."

"Idiot! They almost killed me out there! Where were you?"

"I-I was in back getting the tape recorder

working. Carl, he was yelling at me, and I didn't hear—"

"Never mind!" the major raged. "Get out there now and tell them we'll open the gates in ten minutes. Line them up behind you, and tell them I won't interview anyone from inside city limits so there's no sense in those people waiting!"

Hubert obediently lumbered to the gates. As he opened them a howl went up from the crowd gathered outside again. They surged forward until they saw the huge man, then stopped short. The major grinned as Hubert herded them into line.

"It's amazing how Hubert stops trouble just by appearing!"

"He could stop me making trouble," Bob said.

"He could stop a tank!" Pete declared.

"I expect he could," the major snorted, "if he didn't fall over his own feet! All right, boys, follow me."

The major led them into the center shop and through the empty outer room into a small back room. It's windows looked out on an overgrown backyard and the high rear wall beyond. The windows were closed and an air conditioner purred below one of them. Other than a desk, a telephone, and a few folding chairs, the room was completely bare. A stocky, dark-haired man was busily working a tape recorder that had been set up on the desk. He wore rough work clothes.

"While Carl finishes setting up the recorder, boys, I'll tell you about the Society for Justice to Buccaneers, Brigands, Bandits, and Bushwhackers." The major perched on the edge of the table where the recorder stood, tapping the table with his riding crop. "The society was founded by my very rich great-uncle as a result of his research into the true life of our ancestor Captain Hannibal Karnes, better known as Barracuda Karnes, a privateer who sailed in the Caribbean in colonial days."

"Gosh," Bob said. "I never heard of Barracuda Karnes."

"Nor," Jupiter mused, "have I. The only famous pirate I know of in that general region was Jean Lafitte."

"There, you see?" the major cried. "Barracuda Karnes was just as famous, and just as patriotic, during the Revolutionary War as Jean Lafitte was during the War of 1812, but history has forgotten Barracuda! Neither Lafitte nor Karnes was a pirate—they were privateers, men who plundered ships of their country's enemies. Karnes waylaid the British vessels and ferried their much-needed supplies to the colonists during the Revolution. Lafitte was a smuggler who pirated only Spanish ships and teamed up with Andrew Jackson to beat the British in the War of 1812. No one knows why some men are remembered and some forgotten, but my great-uncle decided to do something about it. He used his millions to found a society that would publish books and pamphlets proving that many forgotten pirates, highwaymen, and thieves were really misunderstood heroes and patriots like Lafitte and Robin Hood!"

"Well . . ." Jupiter began, dubious.

"You'd be surprised, young man!" the major declared. "For many years my uncle scoured the world for details of such historic brigands. When he died, I decided to continue the noble work. I expect California to be a bonanza of undiscovered heroic bandits. Now, if my friend Carl is ready . . . ?" The other man nodded, and the major said, "Well, who'll be first, eh?"

"Me!" Pete cried. "The story of the bandit El Diablo!"

Jupiter, who had already had his mouth open to talk, sat down on a chair next to Bob and grumpily listened to Pete start the story of the Mexican bandit who had attacked the American invaders after the Mexican War. But Pete barely got beyond a description of who El Diablo was before the major broke in.

"Fine! El Diablo sounds like an ideal candidate for a publication by the society. Now, who's next?"

Jupiter didn't wait. "I have two candidates, Major! The French privateer Hippolyte de Bouchard, and his henchman, William Evans, who returned much later as the Purple Pirate! De Bouchard was a French captain in the pay of Argentina, which was at war with Spain back in 1818. With the 38-gun frigate *Argentina*, the 26-gun *Santa Rosa*, and 285 men from ten countries, he was sent to attack Spanish ships and colonies. He was much stronger than the colonials of Alta California, so he burned Monterey, defeated Governor Pablo Sola, and came down to attack the Los Angeles area where—"

"Good! Very good," Major Karnes cried and turned to Bob. "And now, what do you have, boy?"

Cut off so suddenly, Jupiter blinked in disbelief at the little major. He and Pete looked at each other as Bob began to tell about the soldiers of General Fremont who had tried to steal the Cortés Sword from Don Sebastián Alvaro.

"Great! Another good story," the major interrupted. "You boys have done well. Carl has it all on tape, and when we've reviewed everything, we'll contact you."

"Contact us?" Pete said in dismay.

"B-b-but," Jupiter stammered, "your ad didn't say . . ."

The major beamed. "We'll decide which stories to use and then call you for the full interview at twenty-five dollars an hour! A pretty penny for you boys, eh? On your way out tell Hubert to send in the next candidate."

Dazed, the boys went out to the gate and told Hubert what Karnes had said. Slowly they walked past the crowd waiting in line outside the wall and found their bikes. It was Pete who said what they were all thinking.

"Guys, we've been cheated!"

Bob fumed, "That flyer said anyone with a story got paid!"

"It certainly implied that, Records," Jupiter agreed.

"We should report him!" Bob cried.

"I'll bet it was because we're kids," Pete said.

"You're right," Bob decided. "He'll listen to the adults!"

"If he does, then we *will* report him," Jupiter said grimly. "I think we'll go watch Major Karnes and his friends. Come on!"

3

Bob Guesses Wrong

Leaving their bikes still locked to the railing, the Three Investigators ran around the block to the back wall of the courtyard. Bob and Pete climbed quickly up the rough stucco wall and gave a hand to a puffing but determined Jupiter. They were now behind the row of stores. In the overgrown rear yard they found a hidden spot between a gnarled old oak and a spreading jacaranda tree from where they could see into the major's back room. Major Karnes and Carl were already interviewing another boy. The closed windows and humming air conditioner kept the Investigators from hearing the conversation, but they could easily tell what was happening.

"Look!" Pete said softly.

The Investigators saw the boy in the room suddenly look startled, begin to protest, and then slowly leave the room as Major Karnes urged him out. It was just what had happened to them.

"Then it's not only us," Bob realized.

All at once Jupiter started. "Fellows! Watch that man Carl!"

"Watch what, First?" Pete said, peering toward the windows.

"When the next interview ends," Jupiter said.

Bob and Pete watched as a teenager entered the room, talked briefly, and was then hustled out by Karnes. Carl immediately punched a button on the tape recorder. He waited a moment and then punched another button, set the mike out, and, when the next eager candidate began to talk, started the tape moving again.

"He's just rewinding and recording again, First," Pete said slowly. "I don't see . . ."

"Of course!" Bob said. "He's using one cassette over and over! Rewinding the tape and recording again on the same side!"

"And," Jupiter said, "automatically erasing the interview he just taped!"

"Erasing?" Pete said, gaping. "You mean nothing we told them is recorded? It's been erased?"

"Nothing anyone told them is recorded, Second!"

"Then how's the major going to decide who he wants to come back for the interviews that pay?" Pete wondered.

"He can't," Bob said. "Not from what we said, anyway."

"Then why is he doing all this?"

"That," Jupiter said, "is a good question. What . . ." He became alert. "An adult's in there, fellows! Let's see if anything changes!"

Karnes greeted the grownup with the same quick smile and nod to Carl to start the tape running. The visitor got no further with his story than the kids had. The major stopped him with the same pat on the back and gentle but firm move toward the door. The man was as startled as the others had been.

"None of them know Karnes is lying, of course," Jupiter pointed out. "They all think they'll be called back to be paid the money."

"So it's all a cheat," Bob said. "But why, Jupe?"

Jupiter shook his head. "I can't think of any reason, Records. It doesn't make any sense to go to all the trouble of printing the flyer, getting everyone to come here, setting up taping sessions, and then just erasing the tape!"

Jupiter, who wasn't accustomed to not understanding something, pinched his lower lip—a sure sign that he was deep in thought. Suddenly the Investigators became aware that two new people had entered the back room. A tall, thin, bearded man in the blue uniform of a sea captain had come in with a small boy a few years younger than the Three Investigators. Major Karnes seemed suddenly eager. He shook hands with the sea captain, invited him and the boy to sit down, fussed over them, then nodded to Carl to start the tape recorder. The major even sat down as the sea captain talked into the microphone with the boy chiming in from time to time. Bob stared at the newcomers.

"I know them! It's Jeremy Joy—he goes to our school—and I guess that's his dad."

"What is he, some ship's captain?" Pete wondered.

"He operates that little tourist attraction up in Pirates Cove," Bob said. "You know, the Purple Pirate Lair."

"I remember," Pete said. "Sort of a real small Disneyland. It's got a boat ride and a kind of pirate show."

Jupiter nodded. "I've heard of it, but I've never been there. I think it's only been open a few years. It's not very well known."

"I guess it's not very successful," Bob admitted. "But Captain Joy is supposed to be a real expert on the Purple Pirate and his story. I remember he talked to our class once."

"Hey!" Pete said suddenly. "The major's leaving!"

Karnes went out of the room, leaving Carl, Captain Joy, and Jeremy still taping. A minute later there was a howl of anger from the street in front. Staying behind bushes and close to the wall, Pete crawled around to the front courtyard to investigate. He returned in a few minutes, excited.

"Karnes and Hubert are sending everyone else away! The major's hanging a big sign on the front gates—NO MORE INTERVIEWS! He's cheating again!"

They saw Major Karnes return to the back room, followed by the elephantine Hubert in his gray uniform. Karnes motioned Hubert to silence and sat down to listen to Captain Joy.

"Gee," Pete said, "they're sure letting Captain Joy tell his story!"

"Jupe!" Bob exclaimed. "That's it! Captain Joy's an expert on the Purple Pirate. All the society wants is the story of the Purple Pirate, and that's why Karnes doesn't need any of the other interviews."

"No," Jupiter objected. "I tried to talk about the Purple Pirate, remember?"

"Maybe he didn't hear you, Jupe," Pete suggested.

"Or didn't care," Bob added, "because he

knew Captain Joy was an expert on the Purple Pirate."

"Then why not just go to Captain Joy and offer to buy his story?" Jupiter wanted to know.

"Well," Bob said, "I . . ."

"To save money, First," Pete said. "My dad says people often run contests to get something cheaper than they could if they'd just tried to buy it. Everybody likes to win—or make easy money. I'll bet Bob's right—the major set up the whole interview idea just to get Captain Joy's story!"

"That could be the answer," Jupiter said slowly.

His voice was grudging. The pieces didn't quite fit. But he said nothing more as the boys continued to watch Captain Joy and Jeremy talk into the recorder microphone inside the back room. It was about 11:30 when Captain Joy looked at his watch and then got up from his chair. Major Karnes took some money out of his pocket and handed it to the captain, who seemed to refuse it several times and then reluctantly accepted it. Then Karnes shook hands vigorously with the tall man and patted Jeremy on the head. They all left the back room with Karnes talking and beaming with enthusiasm. Quickly the Investigators slipped behind the bushes around the wall to the front courtyard.

They watched through the opened gate as Captain Joy and Jeremy walked out to a battered old pickup truck parked across the street. The truck was painted purple and lettered in gold: THE PURPLE PIRATE LAIR—*Be a Pirate for a Day!* The captain turned to face the courtyard entrance, where Karnes and the others were standing. "I'll see you tonight then, about nine o'clock," he called. Then Captain Joy and his son drove off in the purple pickup.

"Tonight?" whispered Pete.

"Karnes must have wanted the whole story of the Purple Pirate," guessed Bob.

"But—" began Jupe.

Carl started up the motor of the small truck parked in the courtyard and drove out. After shutting the gates behind him, Major Karnes and Hubert walked back into the store.

Bent over, the boys ran back through the bushes to their hiding place behind the stores. They could see Karnes and Hubert studying some kind of document or picture.

"It looks like a diagram or blueprint," said Bob.

Before they could get a closer look, the boys heard a car drive into the courtyard. A new man came into the back room of the empty shop. The newcomer was small, fat, and completely bald, and he sported a big black mustache. He excitedly hurried over to Major Karnes and began to point to something on the document. Soon Karnes and the newcomer were laughing and even Hubert looked happy.

Unable to hear through the closed windows, the boys watched in frustration as Karnes went to the tape recorder and rewound the cassette.

"Jupe?" Pete said. "Isn't that the cassette Captain Joy and Jeremy recorded on?"

Both Jupiter and Bob stared at the Second Investigator, then quickly looked back at the major. He was still rewinding the cassette.

"It has to be!" Bob exclaimed. "That Carl left the cassette on the recorder, I remember! No one was in the room after Captain Joy left until the major and Hubert came back, and they didn't go near the recorder until just now!" He blinked at his companions. "The major's erasing Captain Joy too!"

"Which means," Jupiter said, "that they don't even want the story of the Purple Pirate."

"But they let Captain Joy talk for over half an hour," Pete said.

"And sent away everyone else," Bob said.

"So whatever they do want," Jupiter said, "has something to do with Captain Joy and Jeremy."

"But what do they want?" Bob exclaimed.

"What's going on anyway?" Pete wondered.

"That," Jupiter said grimly, "is what we have to find out. My stomach tells me lunchtime is approaching. Let's return to the salvage yard for something to eat. This afternoon we'll watch Major Karnes and his friends, and we'll talk to Captain Joy." Jupiter grinned at his fellow detectives. "The Three Investigators have a new case!"

4

The Purple Pirate Lair

But the Three Investigators were in for a surprise. To their dismay, Uncle Titus insisted that Jupiter go with him on an overnight buying trip all the way to San Luis Obispo. Bob had to work unexpectedly long hours at the library when a staff member called in sick. And after catching up on his neighbor's yard work, Pete found himself assigned to a long-postponed garage cleanup at home. Thus, it was a full two days later when the frustrated boys gathered in their hidden trailer headquarters just after 11:00 a.m. to begin their investigation into the strange doings of Major Karnes.

"I went by that empty store last night," Jupiter

reported, "and Captain Joy and Jeremy were there, recording their stories."

It was quickly decided that Pete and Jupiter would bike out to Pirates Cove and Bob would return to the shop on De La Vina Street to watch Major Karnes and his cohorts. Bob would carry the First Investigator's latest ingenious tool.

"It's an invisible trailing device," the stout leader explained. "We can follow someone even if he's out of sight!"

Pete examined the small unit dubiously. About the size of a pocket radio, it was a metal container filled with a thick liquid. A tube at the bottom narrowed to a hollow point like an eyedropper. There was a small valve in the tube and a magnet on the side of the container.

"What does it do, First?" Bob asked.

"It leaves a trail invisible to anyone except us. The magnet attaches it to any metal vehicle. The liquid in the container is invisible until you shine an ultraviolet light on it. There's a special valve in the tip that releases a single drop at regular intervals, leaving a trail that can be easily followed by someone with an ultraviolet flashlight."

"And we," Bob guessed, "now have an ultraviolet flashlight?"

"Of course," Jupiter said, grinning. He handed Bob a small flashlight with an odd-looking bulb.

"Uh, guys? What is ultraviolet light?" Pete said, looking sheepish. "I must have missed that class or something."

"It's light with a wavelength shorter than the light we can see, Pete," Bob explained. "People sometimes call it black light because it makes special materials glow iridescent in the dark. If you shine it on the special material in a dark room, you can see the material glow but you can't see the light beam itself."

"I remember now. The other light we can't see is infrared, right?" Pete said. "Does your gimmick work in daylight, Jupe?"

"Yes, but the trail doesn't glow as much, which is probably better," the First Investigator said. "Bob can attach the container to the major's car and follow the trail on his bike. The liquid will keep dripping at regular intervals for approximately two hours."

"Then what are we waiting for?" Bob said.

Bob packed the trailing device and flashlight in a small backpack, and then the three boys crawled out through Tunnel Two and got their bicycles. Bob rode off into town while Pete and Jupiter headed north toward the city limits and the ocean. Jupiter thought aloud as he and Pete biked.

"I doubt it is a coincidence, Second, that Major Karnes asked only those outside the city limits to tape their stories."

"Another setup to fit the Joys, right?"

"It seems most likely," Jupiter agreed.

Pirates Cove was a shallow indentation in the coastline several miles north of Rocky Beach. There was a small village of a few houses and shops, some fishing boats, and an air taxi service along the upper part of the cove. The tourist attraction was on the lower part. As the boys biked up the road along the cove, a crude sign announced THE PURPLE PIRATE LAIR: *An Exciting Adventure for the Whole Family!*

They found the tourist attraction just past an abalone factory. The Lair was on a small peninsula in the cove, with a ramshackle wooden fence enclosing it on the land side. Outside the fence were two parking lots. Across the road to the boys' right, was a thick grove of trees with a fence beyond.

Only a few cars were in the dusty parking lots this early in the day. Several couples sipped soda and waited near the ticket booth outside the gates while their unruly young children kicked each other and screamed. A wooden sign over the booth said "BLACK VULTURE" SAILS AT 12, 1, 2, 3, 4 DAILY. Inside the booth was a stocky man with a weathered face. It was difficult to tell his age, since his skin looked wrinkled beyond its years by constant exposure to the wind. He wore a striped sailor's shirt, a black eye patch, and a red bandanna around his head, and was announcing the thrills of the ride.

"Shiver me timbers, ye landlubbers, everyone's a pirate for a day at the Purple Pirate Lair! Sail across Pirates Cove under the skull and crossbones on the sinister square-rigger the *Black Vulture* if you dare! Battle among the islands! Smell the gunpowder and see the pirates attack! Only a few tickets left! The *Black Vulture* sails in twenty minutes! Don't be left behind!"

The families peered around at each other as if wondering who had bought all the tickets, and then straggled into line at the booth. Pete and Jupiter joined them. When Jupiter reached the ticket window, he spoke firmly to the husky ticket seller, his voice low and very serious.

"We must speak at once with Captain Joy, my good man. An urgent matter."

The ticket man's one visible eye glared at Jupiter.

"Cap'n don't talk to no one durin' a show!"

"But," Jupiter protested, "the show hasn't—"

"Cap'n's aboard! Anna!"

And with that the blustery sailor disappeared

out the back of the booth, and a teenage girl came running in to take his place. She had olive-colored skin and straight black braided hair.

"How many, please?" she asked the boys in a heavy Spanish accent.

"We need to locate Captain Joy at once, miss," said Jupiter.

"No understand. Two tickets, please?" the girl asked uncertainly.

"Swell work, Jupe," Pete said. "What do we do now?"

"I suggest we purchase our tickets and go on the ride. We might get to speak to Captain Joy, and we may learn something about our mystery."

After buying their tickets, Jupe and Pete moved through the wide double-wire gates into a broad central promenade between two long, low frame buildings. The promenade led up to a dock where the *Black Vulture* was tied, with its gangplank down ready to board. The ship was a full-sized replica of a two-masted square-rigger, painted all black and flying the black-and-white skull and crossbones Jolly Roger flag from its mainmast. The two low buildings on either side had obviously once been stables or early garages. The building on the left had been divided into three separate stalls, one serving cold drinks and ice cream, the center one selling souvenirs, and the last offering coffee and hot dogs. The building on the right was open along the front and displayed nautical and piratical exhibits—it was a museum. Both buildings flew the skull and crossbones, and another Jolly Roger flapped over the gates. Everything was small, in need of paint, shabby, and rundown.

To the right of the promenade, behind the museum, the boys could make out rows of live oak trees with a boathouse and a stone tower beyond. Just off shore began a chain of four small islands in the cove, none large enough to be habitable. Beyond the islands the boys could see a small seaplane taking off from the air taxi service on the far side of the cove.

"The Purple Pirate Lair certainly isn't very impressive," Jupiter observed.

"Bob told us Captain Joy wasn't too successful," Pete said. "Maybe that's got something to do with what Karnes is up to."

"That is quite possible, Second," Jupiter agreed.

They walked along the broad promenade, glancing at the museum on the right. It held dusty swords and rusty guns, statues of pirates and sea captains crudely molded out of yellowing wax, and shabby costumes that looked more like Halloween decorations than museum displays. As the boys neared the dock of the *Black Vulture*, they saw a small figure in a loose shirt and baggy buccaneer pants.

"Hey," Pete exclaimed, "it's Jeremy Joy!"

The boy didn't seem to notice Pete, but hurried away up the gangplank of the *Black Vulture*, moored broadside to the pier. Captain Joy himself was pacing the quarterdeck at the back of the ship. The slender owner of the Purple Pirate Lair wore a long black coat, high boots, a wide leather belt, and a cutlass. A tricorn hat like his son's, with a red feather sticking up, was on his head. He also had what looked like a steel hook instead of his left hand! He roared down at the tourists coming aboard.

"Yo, ho, ho and a bottle of rum! Get aboard, me hearties, and be quick about it! There's a rich galleon passing, and the tide's right. We'll weigh anchor and sail to pluck that fat prize!"

Jupe and Pete obediently boarded the vessel with the tourists. Suddenly the voices of pirates singing sea songs and emitting bloodcurdling yells boomed out of loudspeakers set in the rigging above the deck, and cardboard figures of pirates with eye patches and knives in their teeth sprang up around the deck. A single sail flapped out on the foremast, and the *Black Vulture* began to move away from the dock. It was obviously motorized.

"Gosh," Pete said. "It sure isn't very real with that canned singing and the motor."

The small knot of tourists on the deck looked around somewhat glumly at the cardboard pirates and single flapping sail. Suddenly the violent sound of wind and surging waves poured from the loudspeakers. With the fake weather sounds, the fierce recorded pirate yells, and the canned singing, the *Black Vulture* put-put-putted out into Pirates Cove.

"Why would Karnes and his gang be curious about this dumb ride?" asked Pete.

"I don't know, Second," said Jupe. "Keep your eyes open!"

5

Bob Makes a Discovery

When Bob arrived at the walled courtyard on De La Vina Street, he found the high wooden gates locked. So he went around the block and climbed over the back wall again. He cautiously crept through the bushes and weeds and peered in at the same rear store window he had watched two days earlier. No one was inside, and he settled down in the bushes to wait.

Fifteen minutes later he heard the heavy wooden gates creak open. A vehicle drove into the courtyard. Soon Major Karnes strode into the back room of the empty store, carrying a paper bag. The small man seemed to be alone. Bob watched him sit down at the desk, take a container of coffee out of the bag, and drink it. When Karnes had finished, he took a folded piece of paper from his jacket pocket and spread it out on the table.

He bent over the sheet with a small ruler and made some measurements. The results seemed to please him. He wrote something in a small notebook. Then he stood and listened, and Bob heard a second vehicle drive into the courtyard. Karnes went toward the door into the front of the shop. Bob crept through the bushes along the side wall to the front and saw yet another vehicle—a large truck—moving in through the gates.

From the cover of the bushes along the side wall, Bob studied the three vehicles now in the courtyard. There was the van that Carl had gone off in two days before. There was a white ice cream wagon. And there was a large truck with a cherrypicker or platform at the back that could be raised and lowered; the name ALLEN'S TREE SERVICE was on the side. Major Karnes was talking in an undertone to two drivers—an ice cream vendor in a white uniform and a tree-care man in work clothes, with tools hanging from his heavy leather belt. Both of the newcomers had their backs to Bob, but there was something familiar about them. Bob was wracking his brain, trying to think where he had seen the two drivers before, when they climbed back into their trucks and drove out of the courtyard, leaving the wooden gates open.

Major Karnes went back into the empty store. Bob left his hiding place in the bushes and crept up to the front of the shop. He heard the major's raised voice through the open front door.

"Yes, all right, you dolt! I'll give you ten minutes."

Bob heard the telephone slam down. Quickly he took Jupiter's trailing device from his backpack and hurried to the van still parked in the courtyard. He reached under the van and stuck the magnet on the inside of the steel frame, the dropper of the container pointing down. Then he jumped back into the bushes and waited again. He didn't have long to wait this time.

The little major came hurrying out of the empty store, got into the van, and drove through the gates. Outside he stopped, got out, and locked the gates. Then Bob heard the van drive away. He raced to the back wall, scaled it, and found his bike where he'd locked it to a telephone pole. Pedaling hard, he rode back to the wooden gates, then switched on the small ultraviolet flashlight.

The trail of luminous purple dots was clear and led off to the right! Bob grinned and started out in pursuit.

The purple dot trail turned toward the ocean and then toward the freeway. Bob became worried. If Karnes went onto the freeway, there was no way Bob could follow him on a bicycle. That was a mistake in Jupiter's thinking about the new device. Or was it? Bob could hear the stout First Investigator saying that, obviously, if someone they were trailing took the freeway, they were probably going too far to be followed on a bicycle anyway! And as Bob grinned to himself at Jupiter's imagined explanation, he saw with relief that the dots turned away from the freeway and directly into a large shopping center.

Bob rode slowly among the hordes of parked cars in the shopping center lot, looking for the van. Feeling a little foolish to be shining a flashlight on the ground in broad daylight, Bob was relieved to see that most of the shoppers were inside the stores. But he couldn't spot the van anywhere. He continued to follow the trail of dots until they vanished around the corner of a hardware store. Dismounting, Bob peered warily around the corner. The van was parked at the side door of the store, its rear doors wide open. As Bob watched, Karnes came out of the hardware store followed by the enormous Hubert. Hubert was carrying what looked like an armful of old potato sacks.

Hubert stacked the sacks inside the van, and then the two men returned to the store. Bob was aching to look inside the van, but it was too risky to try it when the major and Hubert might reappear any minute. And they did! This time Hubert trotted after his jaunty little boss with an armload of what looked like large flashlight batteries. He put those inside the van, too, and closed the doors.

"Step on it, you moron," snapped Karnes. "I need something to eat."

Both men climbed into the cab of the van and drove away. Frustrated, Bob waited till the van was out of sight so the major would not see him and recognize him. Then he followed the trail of ultraviolet paint once more. He was pedaling rapidly when he rounded another corner of the parking lot and almost ran straight into the rear of the van! Gulping, he looked quickly around for the major and Hubert. The van was parked in front of a fast-food restaurant, and Bob saw the two men inside ordering at the counter. Now was his chance!

He opened the rear doors of the van and stared inside. He saw the piles of old potato sacks. He saw the flashlight batteries. And he saw a pile of shovels and pickaxes, crusted with dirt—fresh dirt from recent digging!

6
A Pirate Attacks!

As the *Black Vulture* chugged across Pirates Cove, Captain Joy's voice boomed out of the loudspeakers along with the sounds of wind and waves and the yells of the pirates.

"Welcome to the Purple Pirate Lair, the biggest, most spine-tingling learning experience north of Los Angeles! You will relive the infamous history of the Purple Pirate of Pirates Cove and his equally villainous associates. Our story begins in the year 1818, when two black ships dropped anchor off the coast of Alta California. They were the 38-gun frigate *Argentina*, under the command of the French privateer, Captain Hippolyte de Bouchard, and the 26-gun *Santa Rosa*, commanded by the pirate Pedro Conde and with a certain Lieutenant William Evans as second in command.

"The ships had 285 men aboard and flew the flag of Argentina. In 1818, Argentina was at war with Spain and had hired these infamous pirates to attack Spanish towns and ships. California was Spanish in 1818, so at dawn on November twenty-first the two ships opened fire on Governor Sola and the town of Monterey."

BOOM!!

"Yipes!" Pete cried. He jumped a foot into the air as a single cannon beside him boomed out a cloud of smoke. The smoke billowed across the deck and everyone began to sneeze.

"The shore batteries soon answered the cannonade!"

"Achoo!"

POP!

The *Black Vulture* was approaching the first of the four small islands in the cove. Jupiter and Pete could make out flimsy walkways connecting the islands to one another and to the shore. As the ship passed the first island, four ragged cardboard figures of old-time Spanish soldiers sprang up out of the brush on some automatic mechanism that made them bob back and forth. A tiny old cannon on shaky wheels wobbled out of the island rocks and fired a second shot. POP!

"A violent artillery duel followed!"

BOOM! The ship cannon billowed its smoke again. POP! The tiny shore cannon wobbled and nearly collapsed.

"Soon the fierce de Bouchard landed an overwhelming attack force that put Governor Sola and his troops to rout!"

From the bowsprit of the slowly moving *Black Vulture*, two pirates swung on ropes to the tiny island, wooden knives in their teeth. On land, they drew cutlasses, shouted nautical oaths, and attacked the cardboard figures, which immediately flopped back down into the brush. The pirates, obviously the weatherbeaten ticket seller and young Jeremy in costume, unfurled a paper Jolly Roger and waved it in triumph.

"I'm beginning to see why Captain Joy isn't doing so good," Pete said.

"Yes, so am I," Jupiter said dryly.

The loudspeaker boomed on. "The pirates burned down every casa in Monterey except the mission and the custom house and then sailed south. Soon they reached Refugio Cove and the Ortega hacienda. The Ortegas put all their wealth into trunks and fled over Refugio Pass to the safety of Santa Ines Mission."

The *Black Vulture* had reached the second tiny island, and now two figures appeared out of its brush, wearing cowboy hats and vests. Obviously Jeremy and the old ticket seller had raced over the walkway from the first island and were now playing the parts of Spanish noblemen. They proceeded to carry a single trunk over a tiny hummock of the island while the loudspeaker blared the sounds of a galloping army and the shouts of a horde of pirates.

"The pirates swarmed ashore and set fire to the entire Ortega hacienda."

Back in pirate costumes, the ticket seller and Jeremy appeared carrying fake torches made of broom handles with red light bulbs glowing on the top. A smoke bomb emitted some thin smoke, painted cardboard ranch buildings flickered red from an obviously revolving wheel, and the two pirates capered grotesquely around the fake fire.

"The two ships continued on down the coast, burning and pillaging, until they reached the cove we now sail, then known as Buenavista Cove. Here the great Spanish landowners were determined to make a final stand to save Los Angeles and the other towns all the way down to San Diego."

The ship was now abreast of the largest of the islands in the cove. A whole host of cardboard figures painted in various old Spanish costumes sprang up all along a low ridge. The painting was crude, most of the colors had faded, and many of the figures were broken. An equally bedraggled set of cardboard pirates bounced up along the shore, and the ship's loudspeakers began to emit battle sounds. The "battle" went on for some time, with recorded cannon fire, pirate yells, brave Spanish defiance, and clashing of swords, while the small throng of tourists on board stared morosely at the pathetic event.

"They fought bravely, those old hidalgos of Alta California, but the pirates won, and this cove has been known ever since as Pirates Cove. De Bouchard and his cutthroats sacked all the haciendas, taking jewels and silver and gold, and then sailed on south to plunder every town they passed until finally sailing away and never returning. But they left behind more than the name of a cove and burned haciendas. They left the Purple Pirate!"

Captain Joy pointed dramatically toward the last island. There, high on a cement block, stood an imposing figure waving a bare cutlass viciously at the air. Thick and stocky, the figure was dressed all in purple—from its broad pirate hat with a tall purple plume to its purple suede boots. The man wore a long purple cloak with gold braid along the edges, baggy purple pirate pants, and a purple mask above a fierce black mustache. He had a brace of old pistols in his purple belt, and a dagger in his boot.

"Lieutenant William Evans, second in command of the *Santa Rosa,* mutinied against de Bouchard, murdered Pedro Conde, and sailed back to Pirates Cove. Here he set up a pirate base, renamed his ship the *Black Vulture,* and terrorized the coast for many years. Always he wore purple, from plume to boots, and thus earned the infamous name of the Purple Pirate. He plundered far and wide, on land and sea, and defeated every military force set against him. He escaped repeatedly from his stone tower fortress, which still stands here at the Purple Pirate Lair—you see it there on your right—until one day in 1840 he was hopelessly trapped in it. Only he wasn't! He just vanished and was never seen again! The Evans family still owns the peninsula and the tower today."

As Captain Joy told the story of the Purple Pirate, the pirate ship turned around and sailed back past the small islands. The boys followed Captain Joy's outstretched arm to see again the old four-story stone tower off to the side of the tourist attraction. It looked remarkably unexciting and empty. Then the whole seedy show was repeated to illustrate the raids and battles of William Evans. The ticket seller and Jeremy played all the parts not taken by cardboard figures, running across the catwalks between the islands to keep up, until the lame show finally ended back at the dock. At that moment one of the air taxis from across the cove roared off overhead to ruin what feeble illusion there had been.

"That completes our ride, ladies and gentlemen, and our tale of the infamous Purple Pirate of California. You will find a refreshment and souvenir stand on your right as you leave the ship. Feel free to take as much time as you need. The next ride will be in fifteen minutes."

There was some laughter and some muttering, but most of the small crowd filed down the gangway in silence. A few paused at the souvenir stand to look among the ship models, daggers, miniature cutlasses, and other plastic junk from Hong Kong. The Mexican girl had closed the ticket booth and was now running the concession stand. Some of the kids made their parents buy them Cokes and hot dogs. Pete and Jupiter waited for the captain and Jeremy, peering into the stands and down the promenade, but the Joys did not reappear.

"I'm sure they live on the grounds," Jupiter said.

They looked behind the shabby museum

building. There was nothing on that side but the stone tower and oak trees. But on the other side of the promenade, behind the refreshment and souvenir stands, they saw a large house trailer. They hurried over to it. A card on the door read CAPTAIN MATTHEW JOY. Jupiter knocked. There was no answer.

"Maybe the captain's still on the ship," Pete suggested.

"I doubt it, Second," Jupiter declared. "Perhaps he's inside and doesn't hear us."

The front windows of the trailer were covered by venetian blinds, but at the rear, where the trailer faced the cove and the long pier of the abalone factory next door, they found an open window. Jupiter leaned in to see if anyone was inside.

"J-J-Jupe!" Pete stammered.

Jupiter whirled from the window. The Purple Pirate stood glaring at them. Suddenly, with a loud cry, the masked pirate raised his cutlass and charged!

"Ahhhhhhhhhhhhh!"

"Help!" Pete cried.

The boys were pinned against the metal trailer, the menacing cutlass only inches away!

7

Trouble for Bob

Backed as far as they could go, Jupiter and Pete gulped and stared at the cutlass inches from their chests.

"So, got you dead to rights, eh!" the gaudy figure of the Purple Pirate cried in the voice of the ticket seller. "Smack dab in broad daylight this time too!"

"W-w-we're just looking for Captain Joy, sir," Pete stammered. "We told you at the gate we—"

"Snooping in windows!" the masked man cried. "Sneaking around here at night!"

"At night?" Jupiter said. "This time? Has someone been sneaking around here at night often?"

"You know durn well how often you've been sneaking . . ."

At that moment Jeremy Joy came around the corner of the trailer. He saw the Purple Pirate and the boys.

"Pete Crenshaw?" Jeremy said. "Jupiter Jones? What are you two doing here?"

Pete blurted quickly, "We came to see your dad, Jeremy!"

"You know these two?" the ticket seller in the Purple Pirate costume said, his voice still suspicious.

"Sure, Sam. They go to my school. Put that sword away!"

Reluctantly the ticket seller put his cutlass into its scabbard and removed his mask. "Too dang many trespassers around here the last couple of nights."

"Sam has a suspicious nature, guys," Jeremy said, grinning, and introduced them. "Sam Davis, this is Pete Crenshaw and Jupiter Jones. Salty Sam's my dad's helper and general assistant."

"Salty Sam," mused Jupiter. "That implies you've had a nautical career."

"Spent twenty years in the navy, if that's what you're drivin' at," retorted Sam.

"You mistook us for some intruders, apparently. This is our first visit to Pirates Cove. We came to talk to Captain Joy about Major Karnes," Jupe explained.

"Dad stopped to fix the coffee machine," Jeremy said. "Let's go find him."

They found Captain Joy at the coffee stand, facing a short, angry tourist.

"We've been cheated," the angry man was saying. "This so-called show is a piece of junk! We want our money back!"

"I'm sorry you didn't enjoy our attraction, sir," the captain said quietly, "but you're not entitled to a refund. There isn't a show in the world that someone wouldn't dislike."

The man glared in fury. "You haven't heard the last of this. You're taking money under false pretenses. We'll see what the Better Business Bureau around here has to say!"

He motioned to a woman and a boy and then strode off toward the parking lots. Captain Joy took out a bright purple handkerchief and mopped his brow.

"I don't know how much longer we can go on without the money to operate properly," the captain said to Jeremy.

"Maybe we oughta just close 'er up, Cap'n," Salty Sam said. "Save what money you got left."

Jeremy glared at Sam, then turned to his

father. "Gee, Dad, I know it'll all work out."

The captain sighed. "Maybe if Major Karnes keeps us telling stories long enough at twenty-five dollars an hour, we might be able to fix some things and start attracting more customers."

"I know he will, Dad!" Jeremy said eagerly.

"Sir," Jupiter said, clearing his throat. "That's exactly what we came to talk to you about."

"Talk to me?" the captain repeated, frowning at Jupiter and Pete. "Just who are you two boys?"

"Jupiter Jones and Pete Crenshaw, Dad," Jeremy said. "From my school. They want to talk to you about Major Karnes."

"What about the major?" Captain Joy wanted to know.

"About what he's doing!" Pete exclaimed.

"We think there's something suspicious about him, sir," Jupiter explained.

"Suspicious?" echoed the owner of the Purple Pirate Lair, staring at the two boys. "There's nothing suspicious about Major Karnes! Ridiculous! First the tourists and now you! Why don't you mind your own business!"

After discovering the sacks and digging tools in the van, Bob waited until Hubert and Major Karnes came out of the restaurant and drove away. Then he rode after them again, following the luminous trail with his special flashlight. This time the dots led him straight to Pirates Cove!

The trail of dots went past the parking lots and entrance to the Purple Pirate Lair. There were few cars in the lots, and only two customers at the ice cream wagon parked out front. Bob had no trouble following the luminous trail as it passed the ice cream wagon, then led back again across the road. It went along a small woods past where a man was working on a tree, standing high on a cherrypicker on the back of a truck from Allen's Tree Service. The man was almost as high as the stone tower across the road, behind the wooden fence of the Purple Pirate Lair. Bob looked around, but he couldn't see the van, or the major and Hubert, anywhere. The trail of dots led north up the road from the tree truck. It was as if it had stopped at the ice cream wagon, the tree-service truck, and then driven right on and . . .

Bob blinked. Ice cream wagon? Tree-service truck? The two men who were with the major earlier that day! Karnes must have come to Pirates Cove just to talk to them and then had left again.

Bob hid his bike behind a bush and carefully slipped closer to the tree-service truck. He watched the man high on the lift. This time he could see the stocky man's face and dark hair, and he knew why the man had seemed familiar. He was the man named Carl who had operated the tape recorder in the empty store when the Investigators had met Major Karnes! And Bob realized, as he looked across the distance toward the ice cream wagon, that the ice cream vendor was Karnes's other assistant—the small, fat, bald one with the big mustache who had come into the empty store last.

It was undercover stakeout! In disguise! Bob wondered if the bald man had been watching here that first day while Carl and Hubert were at the store with the major. And perhaps Hubert had been watching this morning while Carl and the bald man were talking to Karnes in Rocky Beach. The whole gang could be watching the Purple Pirate Lair twenty-four hours a day!

Suddenly Bob noticed that up on the cherry-picker Carl was using binoculars. He was watching something inside the Purple Pirate Lair, but the fence was too high for Bob to see what it was. Carl went on watching, and Bob made a quick decision. He could pick up the trail of Karnes and Hubert later—he wanted to see what Carl was so interested in.

Bob worked his way back down through the trees until he was opposite the entrance to the

Purple Pirate Lair. Taking a last look at Carl, he saw that the dark-haired man had his binoculars trained away from the tourist entrance and off to the right. Now to enter the Lair without attracting attention! Bob walked casually across the road right past the ice cream truck—the bald henchman of Major Karnes had never seen any of the boys—and up to the gates. The ticket booth was closed, but the gates were open. Bob strolled through and made a sharp right turn toward the rows of old oak trees and the stone tower beyond them.

He reached the trees and stood among them to examine the stone tower. Four stories high, with a flat, parapeted top, the tower stood almost at the edge of the cove on the north side of the peninsula. It was shut off from the road by the same high wooden fence that enclosed the Lair. There was nothing around the tower but open dirt and lawn all the way to the trees and the fence. Down the shore from the tower there was a sagging old boathouse. Bob couldn't see anything Carl might have been watching except the tower itself or the old boathouse. He decided to look at the boathouse first.

The rough-hewn boards of the boathouse were gray and weathered. There was a single window in front, and closed double doors. The whole building was leaning to the left and some boards were falling off. The structure looked as if it had been there since the days of the Purple Pirate himself.

Bob tried to peer in the window, but all he could see inside was the dark shine of water in the gloom. He walked over to the doors and pushed them gently.

Then something hard jabbed into his back!

"Turn around son, very slowly," a deep voice said.

A broad-shouldered, medium-sized man wearing white pants, rope sandals, and a blue T-shirt stood watching him. A man who held a pistol aimed straight at Bob!

8

Captain Joy Says No!

Faced with an uncooperative Captain Joy, Jupiter and Pete felt their spirits sink. They started to walk away from the refreshment stand, but Jeremy spoke up.

"Gee, Dad, I know these guys. I think you could at least hear what they have to say."

"Troublemakers, that's what they are," Salty Sam put in. "I say kick 'em out."

"I've got a business to run," said the captain, "but I'll give you five minutes since you're Jeremy's friends. Sam, get back to the ticket booth. You two come with me." Captain Joy led the boys into his trailer. It was furnished like any house, but everything was smaller to fit the tiny rooms. The captain nodded to a couch and Jupiter and Pete sat down. Jeremy perched on the arm of a chair. The captain watched the boys.

"Well, spit it out. What do you have to say about Major Karnes?"

Jupiter explained all they had seen at the interviews two days before, and told how the tapes of the boys and everyone who followed them were erased right away. He pointed out that Karnes had implied that everyone would be paid, though Karnes had actually paid no one but Captain Joy. Jupiter explained how Karnes had no intention of interviewing all those he had sent home on the first day, or anyone who had been in line after the captain.

"Jupiter, is it?" the captain said. "Well, Jupiter, what's wrong with all that? It's obvious that Karnes knew just what he wanted, so he didn't need to spend much time on the first interviews or keep stories he couldn't use."

"What about the ad saying he'd pay everyone?" Pete said.

"You simply misinterpreted the ad, Pete. Or perhaps the major worded it poorly."

"Why send half the people away without even hearing their stories, sir?" Jupiter asked.

"Too many people that first day, just as he

said. I think his in-town and out-of-town idea was good and fair."

"But Dad," Jeremy said, "if he never interviewed the people in town at all, that sure wasn't fair or even honest."

"Well . . ." The captain hesitated.

"Why send out all those circulars in the first place," Jupiter said, "if he wasn't going to interview most of the people who got them?"

"I expect because he didn't realize that Jeremy and I had all the information he needed. That's your answer!"

The captain's voice was triumphant, and Jeremy looked at the boys questioningly. Had they made a mistake?

"In that case, sir," Jupiter said, "why did the major erase *your* interview tape too?"

"My interview?"

"We saw him do it!" Pete cried.

"Impossible!" The captain looked at them. "What are you two really up to? Coming here and trying to get me—"

"Dad?" Jeremy broke in. "Maybe something *is* wrong, you know? I mean, Pete and Jupiter are detectives, and maybe they're right."

"Detectives?" Captain Joy said sarcastically. "You mean this is all some kid game? Playing detective!"

"No, Dad, they're real detectives. Show him, guys," Jeremy said.

"Junior detectives, sir," Jupiter said, handing the captain a card and a letter, "but we've had some successful cases."

The captain took the papers with a scowl and read them.

THE THREE INVESTIGATORS
"We Investigate Anything"
? ? ?

First Investigator .... Jupiter Jones
Second Investigator .... Peter Crenshaw
Records and Research .... Bob Andrews

The captain snorted and read the letter.

This certifies that the bearer is a Volunteer Junior Assistant Deputy cooperating with the police force of Rocky Beach. Any assistance given him will be appreciated.
(Signed) Samuel Reynolds
Chief of Police

Captain Joy nodded slowly and looked more kindly at the boys.

"I see the chief thinks quite highly of you," he said. "I'm sorry I doubted your intentions, boys.

I know now you mean to help, and anyway, it should have been enough that you are friends of Jeremy's. But I'm certain that you've made some mistake, or there has at least been a misunderstanding."

"But Dad," Jeremy said, "why erase your first tape?"

"If he did, perhaps there was a technical reason," the captain said. "Or maybe he wanted to use a special tape for the real interview, or wanted us to start in a different way. We've been taping for two days now, and I'm sure he hasn't erased those tapes!"

"Perhaps you should check on that, sir," Jupiter suggested.

The captain frowned. "Just what do you think the major is doing, Jupiter?"

"It appears to us highly probable that he set up the whole interview scheme just to reach you and Jeremy, sir."

"But we never met Karnes before! We never even heard of him. There's nothing he could possibly want from us. This show barely keeps us alive, and it won't do that if I don't get some money to improve it."

"How about that?" Pete wondered. "Your land here. Maybe the major is trying to steal your land!"

"I don't own the land, Pete. I lease it from the Evans family."

"Evans?" Jupiter said.

The captain nodded. "The old pirate's family still owns land on the cove."

"I thought he just vanished," Pete said.

The captain smiled. "He did, but he came back later. He even reformed. Only it's more dramatic to have him vanish and become a legend."

Jupiter asked, "What about those trespassers at night?"

"I'm not sure there are any. There have been men walking around at night, but the railroad tracks pass near here and sometimes we get tramps who find our buildings a good place to sleep," the captain explained. "Look, boys, I'm certain that you're wrong this time. There's just no reason for Major Karnes or his assistants to be doing anything involving us. There's nothing he could want from us."

"Dad," Jeremy said, "maybe we should just hire the Three Investigators to find out for sure? I mean, be certain."

"No, and that's final!" the captain said firmly to his son. "Boys, I think you're digging for trouble where there isn't any—and we need the money Karnes is paying. I don't want to risk losing it. I want you to stay away from the major. Is that clear?"

Before the glum boys could answer, an angry voice was heard outside the trailer door.

"Joy! Open the door! I've warned you about trespassers!"

9

The Boys Are Warned

"It's Joshua Evans!" Captain Joy said.

He opened the trailer door, and a broad, stocky man wearing white pants and a blue T-shirt came in. His face was red with rage.

"Joy, I've warned you to keep your people away from my tower! Now I've caught one of them trying to break into the old boathouse, and he tells me he's a kid detective working on some fool scheme for you!"

"Bob!" Pete and Jupiter cried.

"What!" the newcomer said angrily to the two Investigators. He dragged Bob into the trailer from outside. "You know this trespasser, do you? Are they juvenile delinquents too, Joy?"

"No, we're not," Pete said hotly, "and neither is Bob!"

The newcomer glowered at Pete. "No one was talking to you, boy. How do these two know my peeping Tom, Joy?"

"I'm sorry you were disturbed, Evans," the captain said. "All these boys are friends of Jeremy's. They came to see me about—"

Jupiter broke in quickly, "The history of the Purple Pirate, sir. A school project. Bob was probably just trying to find us and wandered inadvertently onto your property. I'm sure he had no intention of disturbing you. But I couldn't help hearing that you live in that tower and your name is Evans. Are you perhaps a descendant of William Evans, the Purple Pirate?"

Joshua Evans cocked an eyebrow at Jupiter. "Brainy kid, aren't you? Well, I don't give a fig about school projects, and I warn you to stay off my turf. There's a stand of oaks between my tower and Captain Joy's sideshow for a reason. Keep out!" He turned to Captain Joy. "I'll let the boy go this time, but in the future make sure your customers and friends stay away from my tower."

"You won't be disturbed further," the captain said.

"I'd better not be," Joshua Evans growled,

then banged the trailer door behind him.

The instant the broad-shouldered man had gone, Captain Joy turned to Jupiter. "Why didn't you want me to tell Evans about your real reason for coming here?"

"I'd rather not discuss unproven suspicions with anyone, sir," Jupiter said. "Besides, we don't know anything about Mr. Evans, and I've always found it wise to keep quiet when you don't know who you're talking to."

"I see," the captain said a little suspiciously.

"He seems very nervous about trespassers," Jupiter said.

"He has every right to his privacy. After all, he does own this place, Jupiter," the captain said.

"Gee," Pete wondered, "how could a pirate own land and leave it to his kids? I mean, in the exact same place where he was an outlaw?"

The captain smiled. "William Evans seems to have been a clever man, Pete. As you heard, he was never captured; he just vanished from the tower that day in 1840. However, he left a wife and children, and he suddenly appeared again in 1848 as a soldier with the American army in the Mexican War! We won, California became part of the United States, and Evans got his land back from the American government as a reward for his war service! You see, no one could prove he was the Purple Pirate. There were no finger-prints then, and since the Purple Pirate had never been caught, there were no portraits and no known identifying marks. Over the years his descendants sold off the land until only the tower and the peninsula were left. I leased my part from Evans' mother before she died. Evans left years and years ago, but the tower was always his, and he returned recently."

Jupiter said, "How recently?"

"About a year ago now."

"That long?" Jupiter said, and he sounded disappointed.

The captain looked at his watch. "It's time for our next ride, boys. Time's up."

"I'll be there in a minute, Dad," Jeremy said and walked out with the Three Investigators. The four boys stood in the early afternoon sun-light and watched the few new customers file through the gates and along the main prome-nade.

"Do you guys really think Major Karnes is fooling us for some reason?" asked Jeremy.

"I'm convinced of it, Jeremy," Jupiter said.

"After what I discovered today, so am I!" Bob cried. "Listen to this, guys!"

He told them all about Carl and Major Karnes's other henchman wearing disguises and watching the Purple Pirate Lair, and how the major seemed to have his men spying all day! He told them about the potato sacks and batteries and digging tools in the back of the van.

Jeremy cried, "We better tell my dad all that!"

Jupiter shook his head. "I don't think it would make any difference right now, Jeremy. He doesn't want to believe us, and we'll need something more definite to convince him. It's time we turned to research for some clue as to what Karnes and his gang could be after. Bob, you research the local history of the Purple Pirate. Pete, you examine the records of Pirates Cove. I will delve into Captain Joy's background. Jeremy, may I enlist your aid in solving this mystery?"

"You bet," said Jeremy eagerly. "What can I do?"

"To start with, cudgel your brain for anything in your father's past that might have brought Karnes to him. The last voyage of the *Black Vulture* is at four o'clock, I believe. When could you join us at my uncle's salvage yard?"

"Uh, about five thirty."

"Good. Is that okay with you both?" Jupiter asked, turning to Bob and Pete.

They nodded.

"Then," Jupiter said, "I suggest we all get to work, and meet at Headquarters at five thirty to make our next move!"

10

Jupiter Sees the Answer!

It was exactly five thirty when Jeremy Joy rode his bike through the main gates of The Jones Salvage Yard. The Three Investigators were no-where in sight. He looked around the piles of old machines and salvaged fixtures from hundreds of torn-down buildings, but he couldn't see anything that looked like a headquarters except the yard office.

"You, boy! What do you want?"

The strong voice was almost on top of Jeremy, loud and booming. He turned and saw a large, powerful woman eying him.

I . . . I'm looking for Jupiter, and Bob, and . . ."

"Well, boy, I'm Jupiter's aunt Mathilda, and

you'll have to wait your turn if I find those scamps first! Gone all day, and just when I do find them in the yard, I turn my back for a second and whooosshh! they're gone again!"

"They were here, ma'am?"

"Not five minutes ago! Those scalawags have built-in radar and know I have work for them five minutes before I know it myself!" Under the gruff manner Jeremy heard a kind of amused admiration. "No way of knowing when they'll appear again—maybe you better come back."

"I think I'll just wait, ma'am, if you don't mind."

"Suit yourself, boy. You'll find Jupiter's workshop over that way, but don't expect them back too soon. They know I'm after them for some work!"

She chuckled and went back into the salvage yard office. Jeremy grinned as he walked through the junkyard. He guessed that Jupiter's aunt Mathilda wasn't as stern as she pretended to be.

He found the outdoor workshop in a front corner next to a giant mound of junk, but still saw no sign of the three boys. He sat down to wait on a large corrugated pipe that jutted out from under the mound. He glanced around the workshop, and . . .

"*Jeremy!*"

It was a hollow whisper nearby! Jeremy

jumped up and stared all around.

"Not out there, in here!"

The whispering voice seemed to come from inside the great mound of junk itself!

"P-Pete?" Jeremy stammered. "Jupiter?"

"Shhhhhhhhh!" the voice whispered straight from the junk heap. *"Aunt Mathilda is after us for work! If she spots us, we'll never solve the Karnes mystery!"*

Bewildered, Jeremy looked all around, high and low, but saw no one anywhere!

The unseen voice laughed. *"Make sure no one's watching, then get down and crawl right into the big pipe."*

Jeremy stared at the big corrugated pipe that vanished into the mound of junk. Sure no one could see him, he dropped onto his hands and knees and crawled into the gaping mouth of the pipe. He could just make out Pete lying on his stomach a few yards in, grinning in the dim light.

"This is Tunnel Two," the tall Second Investigator explained. "We've got other entrances to HQ, but we use this one most."

"HQ?" Jeremy exclaimed. "You mean you meet inside all this junk?"

Pete laughed. "Yes and no. Come on."

Jeremy crawled along the pipe behind Pete until there was a sudden square of light above.

He followed Pete up through a trapdoor into a small, cluttered room. There were chairs, tables, filing cabinets, all kinds of equipment, even a stuffed raven! Bob and Jupiter smiled as he climbed up.

"Why, it's a real room," Jeremy said. "I know, we crawled clear under all the junk to a building behind it, right?"

"Wrong," Jupiter said with a twinkle in his eyes. "As a matter of fact, you're in the exact center of the whole junk pile!"

"B-but how did you get a room under the junk?"

The three boys laughed.

"Easy," Bob explained. "It's a house trailer just like yours, but smaller. We just parked it here and piled all the junk over it."

"No one knows we're here," Pete continued, "but we can see anyone outside through our See-All periscope."

"In here," Jupiter added, "no one can see us or find us."

"And," Pete finished, "in here we're safe from Aunt Mathilda and her work!"

This time they all laughed. Jupiter waved Jeremy to take a seat on the last chair and suggested they get to work.

"Jeremy, have you thought of anything that

happened in your dad's past that explains what Karnes could be after?"

"Nothing, Jupe. I thought about it all afternoon. We've lived in Rocky Beach as long as I can remember, and Dad's never been in trouble or done anything shady. Before that he and my mom lived in San Francisco when Dad was in the navy. After Mom died, we came down here and ran a fishing boat for a while. Then Dad leased the Evans place and made it into the Purple Pirate Lair."

Jupiter nodded. "Yes, that's just about all I found out about your dad. Nothing unusual that I can see. What about the Purple Pirate, Records?"

Bob shook his head. "Not much we didn't hear from Captain Joy at the cove, Jupe. The Spanish were sure the Purple Pirate was really William Evans, but they could never catch him to prove it. They thought they had him trapped in his tower more than once, but he always got away. After he came back with the Americans, he was just another respectable citizen."

Pete said, "There's a lot of stuff on Pirates Cove, a couple of whole books and a lot of articles. Besides the Purple Pirate, lots of other people used the cove as a headquarters—smugglers, highwaymen, and even bootleggers smuggling whiskey during Prohibition. All kinds of crooked things went on, but I didn't find anything about a Joy or a Karnes or even an Evans except the Purple Pirate."

Jupiter frowned. "Well, none of that helps much, I guess. It looks as if the only really important clue is the Purple Pirate himself. We know that the major and his gang have been digging, but we don't know why they're watching the Purple Pirate Lair, or why they set up the interviews with Jeremy's father."

"Maybe they think there's pirate treasure around," Pete ventured, "and they want Captain Joy out of the way so he won't find it before they do."

"Or won't see them find it and claim it," Bob suggested.

"Or," Jupiter considered, "perhaps the captain knows something Karnes needs to know in order to dig in the right place! Even the captain doesn't know what it is, and Karnes hopes that if he keeps the captain talking about the Purple Pirate, sooner or later it will accidentally come out!"

"Or already has come out," Jeremy said.

Jupiter thought. "If the captain has already given away the treasure's location, then why do the interviews continue? And if Captain Joy isn't aware of what he knows, why are Karnes and his gang watching the Purple Pirate Lair around the clock? I think we have to try to find out everything the captain said or says in the interviews, fellows."

"Gosh, I can help you with that," Jeremy said. "I can swipe the tapes we've made, and maybe take a small recorder with me to tape what we say from now on."

"We?" Jupiter said. He stared at Jeremy. "That's right. You accompanied your father last night as well. I, uh, had the store under surveillance."

"Sure I went along, Jupe," Jeremy said, puzzled. "Why not? I mean, the major insisted, you know? He says since Dad's been telling me the stories for years, I can make sure he doesn't forget anything."

Jupiter's eyes were bright. "Am I correct in assuming Major Karnes has never been present at the evening taping sessions?"

Jeremy nodded.

"And where does Sam Davis stay at night, Jeremy?"

"He's got a room here in Rocky Beach."

"Does anyone besides you and your dad live at the Purple Pirate Lair?"

"No. Except Joshua Evans, of course."

"One more question, Jeremy. How long do the sessions usually last?" asked the First Investigator.

"From about nine to eleven," the younger boy said.

"Jeremy, go to the taping session tonight as usual, but make Karnes's cohort turn off the air conditioner and open the window. I'll be on a stakeout outside and must hear what's said."

The other three boys in the trailer looked at Jupe with puzzled expressions.

"I think I know the answer to our mystery," Jupiter said, "and I think we can solve it tonight!"

11

Night Stakeout

It was 8:00 p.m. when the Three Investigators met again in their hidden headquarters to begin carrying out Jupiter's plan.

"All right," the leader of the team said, "Jeremy will go with his father to the taping session at the store. I'll stake out the store so I can observe them. Pete will watch at the Purple Pirate Lair. My new walkie-talkies have a range of about three miles, but it's over five miles from the empty store on De La Vina to the Purple Pirate Lair. So Bob will position himself halfway in between and relay messages from one stakeout to the other! Is that all clear, fellows?"

Bob and Pete nodded, and they all went out to their bikes and rode off to their posts.

• • • •

It was almost dark when Pete rode along the county road to Pirates Cove. He switched off his bike lights just before he arrived and coasted into the grove of trees across the road from the gates of the Purple Pirate Lair. He waited for a few moments until his eyes were totally accustomed to the dark. Then he slowly surveyed the night. He saw that the Allen's Tree Service truck was still parked among the trees across the road from the stone tower. The sharp glow and fade of a cigarette showed that someone was sitting behind the steering wheel and still watching. Pete spoke softly into his walkie-talkie.

"Records. Report to First that the major's helper Carl is still staked out at the Lair."

Almost three miles away, on a small rise above the county highway, Bob bent to his walkie-talkie in the now dark night.

"First? Pete reports that Carl is still watching Captain Joy's place."

Two miles from Bob, Jupiter crouched in the brush behind the windows of the back room of the empty store on De La Vina Street.

"Very well, Records. Karnes, Hubert, and the bald man are here in the store doing nothing at all yet. Tell Second to keep on his toes."

•   •   •   •   •

Hidden in the shadows of the trees, Pete did not need Jupiter's warning, not with Carl only a few hundred yards away. With his back against a tree, Pete sat where he could see the entire area of open parking lots, the gates, the top two floors of the stone tower, and the tree-service truck with its solitary occupant.

Just as the last light faded in the west over the cove a pole lamp came on by the Lair's entrance. Then Pete heard a van start inside the Lair, and Captain Joy and Jeremy drove through the gates. Jeremy jumped out and locked the gates, and then the van drove away. Pete looked toward the dim shape of the tree-service truck. It didn't move—the invisible Carl was still smoking slowly inside the cab.

Pete reported, "Captain Joy and Jeremy just left the Lair. Carl is staying put. He's still watching."

Bob passed Pete's message on to Jupiter. When Bob had signed off, he looked down at the dark road and a few minutes later saw the Purple Pirate Lair van pass on its way into Rocky Beach.

Behind the empty store Jupiter listened to Bob's message and watched the three men inside the back room at the same time. Even before Bob had finished talking, Jupiter saw Major Karnes look at his watch, stand up, and start for the door.

The massive Hubert quickly jumped up and followed Karnes out. The man with the mustache remained behind in the back room.

Jupiter quickly crawled through the bushes around the side of the stores and peered into the courtyard. Karnes and Hubert walked quickly out of the store and got into the van with the sacks and digging tools. The van drove away.

Jupiter relayed this information to Bob. Then he returned to his hiding place in the overgrown rear yard. The bald man was checking the tape recorder, putting on a tape, and setting two chairs at the desk. Jupiter heard a van drive into the courtyard out in front. Soon Captain Joy and Jeremy entered the back room. Jeremy hugged his shoulders as if he were cold and exchanged a few words with the bald man, who reluctantly turned off the air conditioner and opened the window. While the bald man was seating the captain at the desk, Jeremy came to the open back window and peered eagerly out into the night, his eyes searching for Jupiter!

At the opened window Jeremy seemed to suddenly realize that he might give away the whole stakeout. He quickly turned and went back to the table and the tape recorder. The bald henchman didn't seem to have noticed him.

"Mr. Santos," said the captain, "I'd like to listen to the tapes we've already recorded."

"Hey," Mr. Santos said, "sorry, Captain. The major he takes them off to the recording lab, I think."

"Why does he do that, Santos?" Jeremy asked.

"He got to edit them, eh? And he got to make copies for the society directors, you know? Hey, let's get started now, okay?"

Santos sat Jeremy at the desk and pushed the record button on the tape recorder. Then he retreated to a corner near the door and started reading a comic book as the captain began his pirate stories.

The First Investigator sat in the dark bushes watching the captain and Jeremy inside the back room. Where were Major Karnes and Hubert? They had left Carl still watching the Purple Pirate Lair, and had left Santos with the captain and Jeremy as they taped pirate stories for twenty-five dollars an hour. It was a method of payment that gave the captain every reason to take as long as possible to tell his stories. Why? Jupiter had a strong hunch why, and an even stronger hunch where the major and Hubert were going!

• • • •

The single lamp outside the Lair shone on the ticket booth and the locked wooden gates. In its dim light Pete could make out no movement in the deserted parking lots. There was only the waxing and waning of the red point of light inside the cab of the tree-service truck, where Carl smoked and watched. From time to time a car passed on the road, and once an air taxi took off from the cove.

Then a van came slowly and almost silently along the road from the direction of Rocky Beach. It entered the parking lot, turned off its lights, and coasted to a stop outside the locked gates of the Purple Pirate Lair. The door opened, and Major Karnes and Hubert got out!

"Records!" Pete whispered into his transmitter. "The major and Hubert just got here!"

Behind the store on De La Vina Street, Jupiter listened closely as Bob relayed Pete's report. His eyes were excited.

"Just as I guessed, Records! The whole taping session is just a ruse to get the captain and Jeremy away from the Purple Pirate Lair so that Karnes and his gang can dig for something they know is on the grounds, or they think is there!"

Bob's voice crackled low, "Pete says Karnes

and Hubert are just waiting in front of the gates. Now Carl has crossed the parking lot to join them. It looks like Carl is picking the padlock on the gates. The major and Hubert are back in the van and driving inside. They're going real slow, Jupe, very quiet. No lights. Now they're inside. Carl's closed the gates, and now he's going back to the tree-service truck. Pete can't see the van or Karnes anymore."

Jupiter chewed on his lip. "Records, tell Pete to follow them. It's vital that he get inside the Lair."

In the dark of the trees Pete shook his head. "No way I can go through the gates. Carl's up in that hydraulic lift now; he'd spot me for sure. I can't go over the fence either. It's too smooth and high, and Carl'd be sure to see me on it anyway."

"Jupe says there's got to be some way to get inside and see what they're doing," Bob relayed.

Pete's eyes searched the whole area for some way to get into the Purple Pirate Lair without being seen at once by Carl.

"Maybe," Pete said after a pause, "I can circle around the abalone factory. The Lair's fence runs right into the near side of the building. But if I go around to the far side, maybe I can climb onto the pier and then swim across to the Lair. That way Carl couldn't spot me."

In the silence of the night Pete waited for the walkie-talkie to answer. Beyond the fence across the road there was no sound, no light.

"Second," Bob's voice relayed, "it just might work. But be careful!"

12

Ten Sacks Full

Under the trees Pete watched the shadow of the tree-service truck only a few hundred yards away. The glowing and fading point of red light told him that Carl was still up on the hydraulic lift, probably so that he could see over the fence of the Purple Pirate Lair.

The Second Investigator studied the road and the empty parking lots. If he stayed on his side of the road, moving away from Carl until he was opposite the abalone factory, he could race across the road to the side of the factory away from Carl.

Taking one last quick look to make sure Carl was still up in the cherrypicker, Pete went low and fast through the trees and then across the silent road to the far side of the abalone factory. Shielded from Carl, he stood there motionless for some time, listening hard. He saw no movement and heard no sign that he had been spotted.

Pete then slipped along the wall of the building to the point where it met the cove. He struggled up the crossbeams and ledges on the side of the factory until he was high enough to drop over the fence separating the factory from its pier. After catching his breath, he dropped down, thudding softly on the wooden planking. Groping his way through the darkness, he walked a short distance out onto the pier. The black water of the cove glinted below him. The peninsula and buildings of the Lair were dimly visible across the water, some twenty or thirty feet away.

Pete soon realized with a sigh that there was no way to cross that water except to drop right into it and swim. Feeling around along the surface of the pier, he found a long rope used for tying up boats. He pulled it toward him and found that one end was still attached to something stationary. With a deeper sigh and a shiver at the chill of the June night, Pete lowered himself down and down until he reached the surface of the water.

There he hesitated for a long minute, braced

himself for the icy plunge into the black water, and then let go and dropped!

And stood up to his ankles in the shallowest water!

Red-faced, and looking quickly around to make sure no one had seen his death-defying plunge into an inch of water, he waded quickly toward the land of the Purple Pirate Lair behind the high fence.

He trotted low and silent to the dark trailer where Captain Joy and Jeremy lived. There were no signs of life.

He saw and heard nothing around the dark ship, which creaked in its dock. He then moved on down the main promenade between the souvenir and refreshment stand on one side and the nautical-piratical museum on the other side. All the buildings were closed and shuttered now. There wasn't a trace of the major's van.

Pete went around behind the museum building and all the way back to where the bow of the ship towered dark in the night. He bent to his transmitter. "Records, I'm inside the fence and have checked the trailer, the buildings, and the ship—and I haven't seen or heard a thing. Not even the van. I don't get it, but they're just not here!"

After a pause Bob's voice came low in Pete's

ear. "First says they have to be there somewhere, Second. He says keep searching."

Pete groaned, but turned and moved into the
thick live oaks that separated the tourist area
from Joshua Evans' stone tower and rundown old
boathouse. He stood among the oaks, watching
and listening. The only sound was a light wind
and the lapping of the cove water against the
shore. And the only light was from a single
window on the first floor of the tower—a window
that faced the wooden fence at the front of the
Lair.

The Second Investigator whispered into his
transmitter, "There's a light in Joshua Evans'
tower. I'll try to get a closer look."

Pete made his way through the oaks to the
fence and then used the fence for cover until he
came level with the tower. Then he got down
and crawled to the lighted window. Inside,
Joshua Evans was alone, reading in an easy chair.
As Pete watched, Evans raised his head as if to
listen. He did this more than once. Pete became
alarmed. Was Pete making some noise he could-
n't hear himself? He backed quickly away from
the window. His foot hit a watering can which
rolled away, banging in the night.

Pete flattened himself on the ground and
froze!

The tower door opened sharply, and Joshua Evans stepped out into the shaft of light, his gun in his hand! The powerful man looked around quickly. Pete shivered. If Evans came toward him . . .

"Meeeeooooooooowwwwwww!"

A black cat ran out of the darkness and began to rub against Evans' leg. The man laughed and lowered his pistol.

"So it's you, Blackbeard. I must be getting old and jumpy. Inside with you, you rascal."

Evans picked up the black cat and returned inside. Pete wiped the sweat from his forehead. If the cat hadn't appeared . . . He quickly crawled back to the fence and then to the oak trees.

"Tell First that the light in the tower turned out to be Mr. Evans reading," said Pete into his walkie-talkie. "I still can't see or hear anything of Karnes and Hubert. It's as if they just vanished."

Hidden in the backyard of the empty store, Jupiter pondered.

"The van has to be there somewhere, Records!"

The stout First Investigator looked at his watch as he waited. It was already almost eleven o'clock. Bob's whisper came.

"Second says all those old stable buildings have double doors in back, big enough to drive a van through. But if he tries to get inside and the major is there, Pete is sure to be seen."

Jupiter transmitted, "No, it's imperative we not be seen until we know what's going on. What else can Pete do?"

Inside the back room of the empty shop, Santos was opening a paper bag and serving donuts to the captain and Jeremy. Bob relayed Pete's next idea.

"Pete thinks the best thing he can do, First, is to hide near the gates and try to see where the van comes from when the major and Hubert leave."

Jupiter nodded. "That sounds like the best way. I think . . . wait! I think the taping session is over. Yes, it's exactly eleven o'clock and the captain and Jeremy are getting ready to leave."

At the corner of the museum building near the Lair's front gates, Pete lay on his belly and peered up the main promenade toward the dark shape of the *Black Vulture* in its dock. He heard only the wind and the small waves and the creak of ship's wood and metal.

Pete felt himself growing drowsy. Struggling to keep awake, he propped his chin on his hands and blinked his eyes rapidly. Then the van was there, coming straight down the promenade toward the gates with its lights off! He hadn't heard the engine start or seen from which direction the van had turned into the promenade. Pete quickly checked his watch—11:00.

He flattened himself in the shadows as the van stopped silently at the wire gates. Hubert lumbered down and pushed the gates open. The van drove through and stopped to wait for him. As it stopped, its rear doors swung open. Before Hubert got the gates closed the light from the pole lamp at the Lair's entrance gave Pete a clear view into the back of the van. It was loaded with rows of full sacks!

Major Karnes snarled from the driver's seat, "You idiot, the back doors weren't locked! Lock them and get in the van!"

The huge man shuffled quickly to do Karnes's bidding. After closing the van doors, he paused a long moment and stared at the exact spot where Pete was hiding! The boy sucked in his breath and froze.

"You dolt, what's taking so long!" came from the front seat.

Scratching his head, Hubert climbed back into the van. The headlights flicked on and then the van disappeared into the night. Pete bent to his transmitter.

"Records! Karnes and Hubert just left. Hubert may have spotted me. I never saw where they came from or where they'd been, but I got a look into the back of the van. It's loaded with those sacks, and they're all full of something!"

From the bushes on De La Vina Street, Jupiter had watched the captain and Jeremy leave the store and heard their truck drive away. As soon as the Joys left, Santos slammed the window shut and turned the air conditioner back on. Then he rewound the captain's tapes and put one back on the machine to be used for more recording. The whole recording operation *was* some kind of trick.

Now Jupe listened to Bob tell him about the full sacks in Karnes's van. He was excited.

"Full? Then whatever they're after is in those bags! Can Second get a closer look? See what's inside the bags?"

"No, the van's already gone. Pete says Carl is still outside watching, so he'll have to leave the way he came and will meet us later at HQ."

"All right," Jupiter said. He bit his lip. "Records, get here to the store as fast as you can."

Less than fifteen minutes later Jupiter heard a van drive into the courtyard out front. Then Major Karnes came into the back room with Hubert plodding behind him. The major and

Santos stood for some time in conference while Hubert finished the bag of donuts and stared vacantly out into the June night. Jupiter crouched lower behind a bush. Then Santos motioned to Hubert, who followed him out like a reluctant elephant. They were going to change the stakeout at the Purple Pirate Lair, Jupiter was certain.

Jupiter heard a scratching sound on the wall behind him. He spun around in the darkness.

One white hand appeared over the top of the wall, then another. Jupiter searched the ground near him for a weapon. His hand closed over a large branch.

A head began to show over the wall. Hair, eyeglasses . . . eyeglasses?

"Okay, First, I'm here," whispered Bob and silently flung himself to the ground. He crouched beside the relieved First Investigator.

"Am I glad to see you, Records. Take my place here. I'm going to find out what's in those sacks and retrieve our trailing device! If Karnes looks like he's leaving, warn me."

Jupiter crawled away into the silent night toward the front courtyard. Bob watched Major Karnes get up and start to pace the room as if thinking hard. Every few seconds the small man impatiently hit the top of his riding boots with his crop. Jupiter's voice came softly from Bob's walkie-talkie.

"All right, Records. I've got the device and I've looked into all ten bags. Let's go to Headquarters."

"Jupe!" Bob said, almost loudly. "What's in the sacks?"

But Jupiter had already signed off and slipped out the front gates to his bike on the street. Bob hurried to join him, and they rode to the salvage yard. Pete joined them shortly afterward in their hidden house trailer.

Jupiter displayed the badly dented trailing device—now worthless—which had obviously hit an obstacle in the road and gotten bashed in.

"Our funds are too low to buy another," sighed Bob.

"Never mind that!" cried Pete impatiently. "Jupe, what was inside the sacks in Karnes's van?"

"Dirt," Jupe said.

"Dirt?" Pete and Bob said at the same time.

"Dirt and rocks," Jupiter repeated. "Ten sacks full of very dry dirt and rocks."

"But . . ." Pete wondered, "why?"

"So that no one will know that they're digging at the Purple Pirate Lair. They're removing the evidence," Jupiter said grimly. "Tomorrow we go back to the Lair and prove to Captain Joy that the taping is a hoax. Then we find out where Karnes is digging, and why!"

13

A Sudden Alarm

When Bob arrived at HQ the next morning, Jupiter was just hanging up the telephone receiver.

"Pete can't come! His dad told him to quit procrastinating and prune his neighbors' bushes. We'll have to go ahead without him. He'll meet us at the Lair as soon as he can."

Bob grinned. "I'll bet he's as mad as a hornet."

"He did not sound pleased," Jupiter admitted. "I'm not pleased either. It gives us one less person to help find where Karnes is digging, and I don't expect that's going to be easy. We may have to separate while we do our scouting. Let's take all three walkie-talkies along."

After Bob had stuffed the devices into his backpack, the two Investigators went out to their bikes and pushed them through Green Gate One out into the street in front of the salvage yard. Soon they were riding cautiously through the low early-morning fog to the Purple Pirate Lair. Heavy mist hung silently over the deserted Pirates Cove.

"I called Jeremy," Jupiter reported, "and he said he'd make sure his father was waiting for us."

As they reached the open gates to the Purple Pirate Lair, Bob said in a low voice, "That fake ice cream truck's over on the road, and I think Hubert is trying to hide in the trees."

Jupiter glanced over and grinned. "Hubert's there all right. Hidden like a whale in a bathtub! He keeps peeking out to make sure no one can see him."

Inside the fence the boys hurried around the refreshment stand to the house trailer. The door opened before they rang.

"Come in, guys," Jeremy said eagerly. "I told my dad you've solved the case!"

Captain Joy was seated at the breakfast table in the kitchen. He offered the boys some coffee. They declined politely, and the captain studied them over his cup.

"I told you not to bother Major Karnes," he said.

"Yes, sir," Jupiter agreed, "and we haven't. He has no idea we're investigating his activities."

"I hope not," Captain Joy said. "All right, if you've solved your mystery, you might as well tell me about it."

"Jeremy is a little optimistic, sir," Jupiter admitted. "We haven't solved the mystery of Major Karnes's actions, but we have determined that there very definitely is a mystery!" He went on to tell the captain everything they had seen and heard the day before. When Jupe had finished, Captain Joy poured himself a fresh cup of coffee, sipped it, and looked mystified.

"You're saying that the whole thing, the Society for Justice to Buccaneers, Brigands, Bandits, and Bushwhackers, is just a trick to get us away from here so Karnes can dig for something?"

"That, sir, is what we think," Jupiter said.

"But what is it all about? Why watch the place so much?"

"I can't explain the stakeout yet," Jupiter said, "but we have a pretty good idea what it must be about. The Purple Pirate must have hidden some of his loot here at Pirates Cove, and Major Karnes and his gang know that. They may even have a map." He told Captain Joy about the document they had seen Karnes studying and measuring, and pointed out that the gang had been digging for three nights.

Captain Joy was doubtful. "There hasn't been even a rumor of treasure at Pirates Cove in a hundred years. After William Evans returned and died, people did think he might have left some treasure, and they dug up the whole cove. But they found nothing, and no one's ever even mentioned the idea since."

"Possibly it isn't treasure," Jupiter agreed, "but Karnes and his gang are digging for something, sir! Whatever it is, I suggest we try to find where they are digging."

"Good grief, there should be a big hole after three days," Jeremy exclaimed.

"Then it should be simple to find," Captain Joy said.

"I wonder," Jupiter said uneasily. "If removing the dirt would hide the digging, then the hole is not in plain sight or where anyone can stumble onto it by sheer chance."

"I'll go with Jeremy," Bob suggested, "and you go with the captain, Jupe. They both know the grounds."

Jupiter nodded. "For a start, you check the whole area between the refreshment building and the cove, and we'll start inside the refreshment building."

They agreed to meet near the *Black Vulture*.

As Jupiter and the captain entered the rear area behind the refreshment stand, the early-morning fog drifted in with them.

"This building and the museum building were stables originally, back when there was a big house over there in the trees. That was long before the cove road was built," the captain said. "Both buildings still have double doors for each separate stall. Plenty of room to drive a van in."

He unlocked the first pair of double doors. Inside, cases of soft drinks and boxes of food were stacked to the ceiling. There was enough room to hide a van, but there were no traces of tire marks or signs of digging in the dirt floor. They had no better success in the areas behind the other two sections of the refreshment stand, and soon joined Bob and Jeremy beside the *Black Vulture*.

"Nothing," Bob reported. "We searched every inch of ground from building to water."

They decided there was no way to drive a van onto the *Black Vulture*. Captain Joy suddenly looked at his watch.

"Hey, it's time to open. Salty Sam seems to have wandered off, so Anna will have to take care of the ticket selling. If we get a good crowd I may hire you boys to do some acting."

Jupiter's eyes lit up. "As it happens, sir, I have considerable experience in that line. I may even decide to return to acting when I grow up instead of becoming a great detective."

"Meanwhile," Bob said, grinning, "we're trying to find where Karnes and his gang are digging. May we borrow your keys to the museum, Captain Joy?"

The captain willingly handed over the keys and then hurried off with Jeremy to start the first show. After the Joys had gone, Bob and Jupiter crossed the promenade and unlocked the first set of rear double doors in the museum building. Although the partitions between the old stable stalls had been torn down in front to make the long museum display, there were still three separate dim rooms in back.

"Look for tire marks and digging," Jupiter emphasized.

In the first room they found nothing—no tire marks, no loose dirt, no hole in the ground. The second of the dim back rooms was no more rewarding. As they started to leave it, Bob held up his hand in alarm!

Someone, or something, was moving outside in the fog.

Moving stealthily—and coming toward the door!

14

The Purple Pirate Strikes Again

"Quick!" Jupiter whispered. "Behind the door!"

But before they could move an inch, a shadow leaped through the doorway and grappled with Jupiter! The stout leader of the trio and his shadowy attacker fell to the dirt floor in a tangle of arms and legs. Bob leaped onto the assailant's back and all three rolled in the dirt of the dim room.

"I've got his leg!" Bob cried.

"I've got his hair!" Jupiter panted.

"I've got his neck!" Pete groaned.

The three figures slowly stopped moving.

"Pete?" Bob ventured.

"S-Second?" Jupiter stammered.

"Yes," the Second Investigator sighed wearily. "It's me. I just got to the Lair. I heard someone inside the museum and came in to investigate. You want to let go of my hair, Jupe?"

Jupiter stood up red-faced.

"We heard someone sneaking up," Bob explained.

Pete said, "If you let go of my leg, Records, I'll drop your neck."

"A small error on all our parts," Jupiter said. "Didn't the captain or Jeremy tell you we were in here?"

"I didn't see the captain or Jeremy. What's up? Have you found where Karnes and his gang are digging?"

Jupiter shook his head. "But we still have one more room to check in this building."

The boys unlocked the last of the former stable rooms, and the result was the same. There was no sign there of digging.

Out in the thinning fog, the Three Investigators next spread out across the ground between the museum building and the grove of live oaks that separated the Purple Pirate Lair from Joshua Evans' stone tower. They could see a narrow line of customers straggling through the gates toward the *Black Vulture*. The refreshment stand was open now, with the captain himself behind the counter. The three boys searched every foot of ground from the water to the fence and up to the oak trees.

"No one's been digging anywhere here," Bob said.

"Except that Karnes and Hubert *are* digging here," Pete said.

"And it's impossible for both things to be true," Jupiter said.

"Unless," Pete suggested, "Karnes came back last night and filled it all in?"

"We'd see any freshly turned earth," Jupiter said. "No, we've looked everywhere now, and somehow we've missed—"

"Not everywhere, First," Bob said suddenly. "There's still the stone tower and the old boathouse beyond these trees."

They looked through the twisted old oaks at the tower and the tumbledown boathouse standing at the edge of the cove. There were enough gaps among the oaks for a van to drive through.

"But," Pete wondered, "how do you dig in a stone tower or a boathouse? One's stone, the other's water!"

"But you could certainly hide a van in that boathouse if there's enough dock area inside it," Jupiter said. "Come on, Bob's right. We must take a look."

"Hold on," Bob said. "That Joshua Evans was awful mad about me being on his land yesterday. Maybe we better wait for Captain Joy."

Jupiter sighed. "You may have a point, Records."

"Mr. Evans isn't at the tower," Pete said. "I saw him drive away from the parking lot when I was coming in."

"Then," Jupiter cried, "let's go and look!"

As they hurried through the oaks, they saw that Captain Joy was now on the ship, talking to a group of customers and looking at his watch. At the gates Anna still had the ticket booth open. The boys tried the old boathouse first. It had double doors on the land side, and it wasn't locked. Just inside the doors there was room to park a van on the wooden floor, but there was no trace of tire tracks or oil drippings. The dock jutted out into dark water inside the boathouse, with berths on each side for boats. No boats were tied up. At the far end doors large enough to let small boats sail through were closed almost down to the waterline. A sail loft that ran the length of the boathouse directly over the dock held sails, masts, and ropes. Under the dock the water lapped against wood; again there was no evidence of digging.

The boys saw no signs of digging all the way to the stone tower, either.

"Pete," Jupiter decided, "you stand watch in the oaks. Here's your walkie-talkie and the backpack. If you see Joshua Evans returning, warn us. We'll set our instruments on receive."

As Jupiter walked toward the tower, his eyes scanned the outside. The first floor had two doors and several windows. The second and third floors had one tiny window each. The top floor was glassed in on all sides like a lighthouse. Between those windows were a series of projecting steplike stones leading up to the flat roof.

Jupiter tried the front door of the tower. It was unlocked. The door opened directly into a small living room. It looked exactly like most other living rooms the boys had seen except that it was shaped rather like a large piece of pie, with a curved wall. There was a pie-shaped bedroom to the right, and a pie-shaped kitchen to the left. The back outside door was in the kitchen and was bolted shut from inside. Wooden stairs led down along one inside wall from the kitchen to the cellar. On the other inside kitchen wall, toward the tip of the pie shape, a door opened into a kind of vertical well where a ladder went up to the next floor.

"We'll try the cellar first," Jupiter declared.

The went down the worn wooden stairs into the pitch-dark cellar. Jupiter groped for a light switch.

A small ceiling bulb gave only a dim light, but the boys could see that they were in a low-ceilinged, semicircular room with a dirt floor and bare stone walls. The hard-packed dirt of the floor was as smooth and solid as cement, and the stone walls were dry as dust and hadn't been disturbed in a century.

"No one's been digging here," Bob said.

"It would seem that way," Jupiter agreed reluctantly.

A door in a stone partition led into a storeroom filled with massive old furniture covered with dust. The boys looked under the furniture for signs of disturbed earth.

"No one's been digging anywhere in this cellar," Bob finally said.

Jupiter nodded and sighed unhappily.

"*Aaahhhhhhrrrrrrgggggg!*"

They whirled. The Purple Pirate stood behind them! His cutlass shone faintly in the dim light of the storeroom.

"Hey, Mr. Davis," Bob said, annoyed, "it's just us again."

The Purple Pirate said nothing. He stared at them through his purple mask and thick black mustache, his eyes glittering.

"Mr. Davis?" Jupiter said.

The Purple Pirate raised the cutlass and

charged, swinging the great long sword. Bob dove one way over a massive chest, Jupiter the other behind some heavy chairs. The Purple Pirate tripped over Bob's foot and sprawled across two long oak tables, sliding to the back wall.

Jupiter and Bob didn't wait. With nothing but escape on their minds, they ran out of the storeroom and up the stairs into the kitchen. Suddenly Pete's hushed voice seemed to be in the kitchen with them.

"Alarm! Evans is coming back! Alarm, you guys!"

The back door of the tower was locked as well as bolted from inside! The boys could hear the Purple Pirate, whoever he really was, stumbling across the cellar toward the stairs. And outside, in front, Joshua Evans was returning.

They had nowhere to run.

15

Trapped!

Among the oaks in the lifting fog Pete whispered again into the walkie-talkie.

"Alarm! Evans coming, guys! Get out!"

There was no response!

Pete glanced quickly toward Joshua Evans, who was still walking from the gates toward the grove of oaks. There was barely time for the two boys to escape unseen.

"First? Records? Alarm! Get out fast!"

He saw the front door of the tower start to open! They would make it out! Then he blinked. No one was coming out! The door was slowly swinging open by itself, as if Bob and Jupiter had neglected to close it properly. Then Pete saw the black cat. It had pushed open the tower door by itself and was now bounding off toward the cove. But Bob and Jupiter remained inside.

Pete whispered desperately into his walkie-talkie, "Records! First! Evans is—"

"Evans is what, you young punk!"

Pete looked up, straight into the angry face of Joshua Evans!

"So, trespassing again after I warned all of you! Just what the devil are you up to, and who are you talking to on that thing?"

Pete gulped, "W-we're looking for where they've been digging, sir. I mean, we think they're after some treasure or something. Buried around here, you know? We've looked most places. First and Records thought maybe it was in your tower somewhere. I stayed out here as . . . as . . ."

"Lookout," Evans said. He glanced toward his tower and its open door. "Digging, you say." His dark eyes looked down again at Pete. "Just who are 'they'?"

"They?" Pete was confused.

"The people who're looking for something. The diggers."

"Oh," Pete said. "Major Karnes and his gang. Hubert, Carl, and Santos, the bald guy."

Startled, Mr. Evans looked quickly toward his tower again. "But you haven't found where they're digging yet?"

"No," Pete admitted. "We've looked everywhere except . . ."

His walkie-talkie seemed to pant softly. A low, breathing, blowing sound. The silent signal. Pete bent to the unit.

"Jupe? Bob?"

Jupiter's voice came very low. "Someone is in the tower, Second, and he's after us! We got out of the cellar, but we couldn't get out the front without Evans seeing us, and the back door is locked, so the only place we could go was up! We're on the second floor. There are just some old crates and chests in here. . . ." There was a sudden silence. "He's coming up! We've got to go higher!"

The walkie-talkie went dead.

On the second floor of the tower, Jupiter and Bob listened to the slow, heavy steps climbing up the ladder from the kitchen. There were sounds of grunting and hard breathing.

"Hurry," Jupiter said.

By the light from the one tiny window, the two boys tiptoed over to the ladder to the third floor, on the opposite side of the room. They went up quickly, with Jupiter puffing a little. The third floor was another dimly lit room with a few old barrels and dusty wooden crates that looked as if they had been stored in the tower for a hundred years. Jupiter and Bob sat on two of the crates. Below they heard the man in the Purple Pirate costume tramping around on the second floor.

"Who could it be, Jupe?" Bob whispered. "I mean, if it isn't Salty Sam?"

"If it is Sam," Jupiter said, "why would he attack us?"

The boys listened to the slow footsteps below. "Records!" Jupe suddenly said. "I don't think that man down there, whoever he is, is chasing us at all! I think he's just searching the tower."

"He sure chased us out of the cellar!"

"That's true," Jupiter conceded, "but he's not acting as if he were chasing us now. In fact, he's acting as if he doesn't even know we're here. As if he thinks we escaped outside."

"Maybe it's Major Karnes himself," Bob suggested.

Jupiter shook his head. "The man we saw is much too big for Major Karnes, and much too small for Hubert. But it could be one of the other two, Carl or Santos. At least we know it's not Joshua Evans—he's right outside."

Bob nodded. "Jupe! The guy is coming up here now!"

The ladder to the fourth floor ended in a trapdoor. The boys pushed it open and climbed out into a dazzle of light! The fourth and last floor was the smallest but had windows on all sides. Quickly closing the trapdoor, the boys went over to the windows. They could see the cove, the *Black Vulture* still tied up and waiting to start the first show, the ocean, and the sun through the last haze of fog.

"Jupe?" Bob said. "What do we do if he comes up here?"

The ground was far below the windows, and there was no way to climb down the outside of the tower. The bright room had no furniture and no place to hide. There was only the trapdoor below and the roof above.

"I don't know," Jupiter said, and his voice sounded suddenly afraid. "But we have to do something, because I hear him on the ladder right now!"

"He—he's coming up!" Bob stammered.

Among the oaks, Pete and Joshua Evans continued to watch the tower and wait for the silent walkie-talkie to speak again.

"Maybe we should go in and look for them," Pete said.

"What's your name, son?" Joshua Evans asked quietly.

"Pete," the Second Investigator said. "Pete Crenshaw."

"Pete, we don't know who's in there, or if there's more than one. He's between us and your friends. We could put them in more danger than they are now."

"I-I guess you're right. But what if . . . ?"

Evans pointed to the top of the tower. "Look, at the top windows!"

Pete looked up and saw Bob and Jupiter peering out. He started to run forward and wave, but Evans pulled him back, and the boys didn't see him.

"Careful, Pete," Evans warned quietly. "You don't want to draw any attention to your friends."

Pete swallowed and nodded. Bob and Jupiter were no longer at the tower windows anyway. Then Joshua Evans gripped Pete's arm and pointed up at the windows again. Pete saw the purple-masked face with the black mustache, the purple plumed pirate hat, the gold-laced purple coat! The Purple Pirate was on the top floor of the stone tower!

"W-where can they hide up there?" Pete whispered.

Joshua Evans shook his head. "Nowhere, Pete. There isn't a closet, a cabinet, anything. They're trapped!"

16

Jupiter Gets Stuck

Pete and Mr. Evans stared up at the silent tower. The figure of the Purple Pirate had vanished and the empty windows reflected only the noonday sun. Mr. Evans sighed.

"He must have caught them, Pete."

"Then we've got to rescue them!" Pete cried.

"Easy, son," Evans said. "We could make it worse by any sudden action. I think that if we . . ."

"*Second? Has he gone?*" The disembodied voice came up out of the walkie-talkie. "*Did you see him?*"

"First! Where are you?"

"Still at the top of the tower," Jupe said. "Look up and you'll see us."

Evans and Pete looked up again at the top windows of the tower. They saw no one!

"We can't see anyone up there, First!"

Jupiter chuckled. "Higher, Second. Above the windows."

Pete looked again and saw two grinning faces peering over the low parapet at the edge of the roof! Jupe and Bob had climbed out of the windows and somehow up onto the roof of the old tower four stories above the ground.

"How'd you get up there?" Pete demanded.

"The question," Jupiter said with a moan, "is how do we get down!"

Bob broke in. "Second, you said 'we' earlier. Who's down there with you?"

"Mr. Evans," Pete explained. "He's okay, guys."

Evans spoke into the transmitter. "Now that Pete's told me all about what you boys are doing, I certainly want to help find out what's going on around here. Did you two say you thought that the Purple Pirate had left the tower?"

"We heard him go down again to the third floor," Bob said. "We may have heard him go down all the way, but we're not sure."

"Okay," Evans said, "we'd better check it out. You wait."

He and Pete approached the open front door of the stone tower warily. They heard no sounds at all in the tower. The back door was still bolted from the inside. If the pirate had left by the front door, Evans and Pete would have seen him. Mystified, they inspected the dim cellar and then the second and third floors. Whoever he had been, the man in the Purple Pirate costume was gone. Evans and Pete climbed up to the top floor, where Bob came in a rear window grinning at them.

"Where's Jupe?" Pete asked.

"Still on the roof," Bob said, laughing. "He says he can't get down by himself, and I'm sure not strong enough to carry him."

"How did you two ever get up there?" Evans wondered.

"I'll show you," Bob said. He leaned out the same window he'd climbed in through. "See?"

Pete and Joshua Evans leaned out. They saw a series of stones projecting from the outside wall near the window. The stones made footholds and handholds going up from the window to the roof.

"I guess your ancestor had to have a way to reach the roof," Bob decided.

"Jupe got to the roof on those!" Pete cried, gaping.

Bob smiled. "The Purple Pirate was coming up, and we had nowhere else to go. I guess you can do a lot more when you're scared. But no one's chasing Jupe now, and he says there's no way he can climb down."

"Like my cat, Blackbeard, in a tree," Mr. Evans said. "He can get up, but it takes the fire department to get him down."

"Maybe we'll have to call the fire department for Jupe," Pete said, giggling.

"I think a strong rope will do," Bob decided. "Do you have a rope in the tower, Mr. Evans?"

"I sure do. I'll get it."

Evans soon returned with the rope, and Bob and Pete climbed up onto the roof with it. Jupiter stood there in the now bright day looking out at the cove. He seemed to be watching the *Black Vulture* as it sailed by the small islands on its much postponed first ride of the day. Onboard, a larger than usual group of tourists, increased because of the delay, observed the attack of the two pirates acted by Jeremy and Sam Davis.

"Would you say," the stout First Investigator said as Bob and Pete came up, "that someone wearing boots would make noise walking down wooden stairs?"

"I guess so, Jupe," Pete said.

"Usually plenty of noise," Bob added as he uncoiled the rope.

Jupiter nodded. "And you saw no one go in or out of the front door, Second?"

"Only the cat." Pete told them both about the cat coming out just as Mr. Evans appeared. "You guys must not have closed the door all the way."

"That explains why our Purple Pirate thought we had escaped through the front door," Jupiter realized. "Or, to be more precise, why whoever it was thought he had successfully scared us out of the building through the front door."

"Lucky for us the cat was in the tower, then," Bob said.

"Luck," Jupiter said smugly, "is simply planning so well that you are ready to take advantage of events." Then he added, smiling, "But luck sure helps if you can get it!"

"And speaking about help," Pete asked, "you ready to get down from here, First?"

"I," the leader of the trio said, "am not climbing back down on that route for midgets and flies. I'm not at all sure how I got up here, but I know that as far as climbing down is concerned, I am ready to live up here permanently. You may ask Aunt Mathilda and Uncle Titus to send up some food and my bed!"

"We could send for a helicopter," Bob said, "but I think a good rope will do."

"Rope?" Jupiter cried. "Do I look like Tarzan?"

"We just tie the rope around you," Bob explained, "and then you climb down while we hold the rope secure so you can't fall."

Jupiter looked at the rope, then looked over the side of the high tower. He shuddered. "Well, I suppose it's the only way short of living up here forever. Tie on your rope."

Bob and Pete tied the rope firmly around Jupiter's waist and then held it securely, their feet braced against the low parapet of the roof. Jupiter knelt on the parapet, facing them. Taking a deep breath, he gingerly lowered his legs over the side and groped his way down with the small foot- and handholds. Moments later he was helped through the window below by Joshua Evans, and Bob and Pete swarmed down behind him. Once inside, they all hurried down to the first floor.

"You think that Purple Pirate just wanted to scare us out of the tower, Jupe?" Bob said.

"I'm convinced of it, Records."

Joshua Evans said, "Any idea who it was, Jupiter?"

"Well, sir, it wasn't Major Karnes—he's much too short. And his helper, Hubert, is much too big. I considered you a strong possibility —you're the right size—but you were out there with Pete."

"Lucky for me," Evans said with a laugh.

"It certainly rules you out," Jupiter agreed somewhat humorlessly, "along with Karnes and Hubert. But the pirate could be almost anyone else—it's very hard to tell a person's actual size and build in that costume."

"And you're sure he only wanted to scare you away," Evans continued. "Why?"

"To search the tower for something he thinks is hidden in it somewhere."

"Hidden, Jupe?" Bob said. "I thought you were sure Karnes and his gang were digging for treasure or something."

"I'm now convinced whatever they are after is not buried but simply hidden."

"Gosh, Jupe," Pete exclaimed, "then why are they digging?"

"I think," Jupiter said, "that if we all go down into the cellar again, I can tell you exactly why Major Karnes is digging, and where!"

17

A Surprising Discovery

Their footsteps on the wooden stairs echoed loudly through the low, enclosed space of the dimly lit cellar.

"Records," Jupiter said, "do you remember when we first heard the Purple Pirate down here?"

"Sure. We were back there in that storeroom. He growled right behind us, and we turned and saw him."

"Exactly." Jupiter nodded. "So the very first sound we heard was his growl behind us in the storeroom. But we all just heard what a clatter we made coming down those wooden cellar stairs. Why didn't we hear the Purple Pirate in his heavy boots?"

"Maybe he tiptoed real quietly," Bob said.

"It would be hard—those stairs are very loose and creaky," Jupiter said. "But I have another question. For you this time, Pete. Why didn't you warn us when the Purple Pirate came into the tower?"

"Because I didn't see him go into the tower."

"Exactly again," Jupiter said maddeningly. "So you saw no one enter the tower, Bob and I heard no sound of boots coming down the cellar stairs, and the kitchen door was bolted on the inside. I know that because I tested it first thing."

"So?" Pete asked. "What does all that mean, First?"

"It means," Jupiter said, pausing as usual for effect, "that the Purple Pirate who attacked us did not get into the cellar by coming down the stairs from the first floor, and did not get into the house through any entrance on the first floor."

"But there isn't any other way to get into the tower or the cellar," Bob said.

"There must be, Records," Jupiter insisted. "There must be some way of entering the tower and the cellar directly from the outside. And that's why Karnes and his gang have been digging!"

"They're digging a tunnel into the cellar!" Bob guessed.

"No, not digging," Jupiter corrected him. "Probably clearing out. Remember all those miraculous escapes of the Purple Pirate in the old days, fellows? He must have had an escape tunnel out of the tower. Somewhere in this cellar there must be an old tunnel to the outside!"

Joshua Evans said, "Jupiter is absolutely right, boys. There *is* an escape tunnel out of this cellar. It would have to be dug out, I guess. It was supposed to have collapsed years ago. The only thing is, I've never known exactly where it is."

"Then let's find it," Pete exclaimed.

Eagerly the Investigators and Mr. Evans spread out across the cellar and began to study the old walls. They tapped on them with pieces of pipe and boards they found in the storeroom, and looked for any signs of loose stones or hinges.

"Look on the floor for footprints," Jupiter instructed.

But the dry clay of the cellar floor was far too hard to reveal any footprints.

"Here!" Joshua Evans cried.

He struck some stones again as the boys gathered around him. Almost directly facing the stairs, the wall gave off a faint hollow sound. There seemed to be an empty space behind the stones for sound to echo in. But as closely as the boys looked, they could see no sign of a door or of loose stones. Jupiter slowly surveyed the dim cellar.

"The tunnel was meant to be a secret escape route, so its door would be well hidden. But the door would have to open from this side—and open fast. The Purple Pirate would need to leave in a hurry if he needed to use the tunnel at all. He would have to come down the stairs, and he'd want to open the door as quickly as possible. Try the stairs."

They examined every step of the wooden stairs, carefully studying the stone wall above and below. Pete found a small iron ring under a step halfway down. The ring pulled a single flat stone out of the wall. In the space behind the stone was a large, well-oiled iron lever. When Pete pressed the lever down, the section of wall facing the stairs silently slid open!

"Well, I'll be!" exclaimed Joshua Evans. "All this time and I never knew I had a secret doorway right here!"

Mr. Evans got a flashlight from the storeroom and led the boys into a narrow tunnel just wide enough for one man and high enough for Pete to barely stand up straight. On the wall just inside the tunnel was another lever.

"That must be for opening and closing the door from inside the tunnel," Jupiter noted.

The passageway had a vaulted stone ceiling and stone walls and a dirt floor. All along its length stones had fallen from the walls and the ceiling. After some twenty yards the whole tunnel had collapsed.

"My father told me it fell in before I was born," Joshua Evans said. "Probably in one of the big earthquakes."

But the tunnel was no longer blocked. A passage wide enough for even a large man to crawl through had been dug through the debris at the top. The Investigators and Evans crawled through one at a time and emerged on the far side. More fallen stones littered the passage as it continued darkly ahead, and some twenty yards farther on it ended at four heavy, rough-hewn boards with rusted iron cross-braces. The four vertical boards were hinged at the bottom to a timber set in the dirt floor, and attached to beams on either side by two brass bolts.

Pete and Bob slid open the bolts, and the four boards lowered outward like a drawbridge. Everyone walked forward—and Joshua Evans' flashlight glinted on dark, black water! Ahead, the tunnel seemed to continue with wooden walls and ceiling and a water floor.

"We're inside the boathouse under the pier!" Jupiter cried.

"By thunder, you're right," Joshua Evans said.

"The only way out is to swim," Bob added.

"Uh, it's probably shallow enough to walk in," said Pete, red-faced, remembering his experience at the abalone pier.

"We'd better close the entrance to the tunnel behind us," Jupiter said. "We don't want Karnes or anyone else to know we've found it.

Bob and Pete pushed the four hinged boards back up and closed the bolts from the back by sliding protruding wooden pegs into place.

"Gosh, no wonder we missed this door earlier," Bob said. "No one could tell it isn't just four boards holding up the pier."

Joshua Evans and the boys waded out and climbed up onto the pier in the dim boathouse. Only a little sunlight filtered through cracks in the wall and the single dirty window in front. As they walked out through the double doors, Jupiter looked back thoughtfully.

"Bob's right—there's no way anyone could discover that tunnel by accident. Which means that Major Karnes had to know it was there, and perhaps exactly where it was."

"Remember that document he was studying in the store?" Bob said. "I bet it was a map with the tunnel on it."

"Perhaps, yes," Jupiter agreed.

They walked through the grove of oaks to the

Black Vulture, which had just returned from the first show of the day. Captain Joy, Jeremy, and Salty Sam were still on the deck. Captain Joy was alarmed when he saw Joshua Evans with the Investigators.

"I told the boys to stay—"

Mr. Evans smiled. "It's all right, Joy, I know what the boys are doing now. It seems as much in my interest as anyone's to solve the mystery of what this Major . . . Major . . ."

"Karnes, sir," Jupiter supplied, and turned to Captain Joy. "When did you start the first ride today, sir?"

"Only about forty-five minutes ago," the captain said, glaring toward Sam Davis, who seemed very interested in the distance. "Thanks to Sam. We waited for him so long we finally had to start without him, but he arrived at the first island in the nick of time."

Pete could restrain himself no longer. "We found where Karnes and his gang are digging, Captain! And why they wanted you and Jeremy away from your place. There's an old escape tunnel from the tower to the boathouse! They've been clearing it out!"

The boys went on to explain all that had happened that morning, including their pursuit by the man in the Purple Pirate suit.

Jupiter faced Sam Davis. "Why were you so late today?"

"Couldn't get my dang car started, if it's any of your business, young feller," the hefty sailor said. "Got so late I just skedaddled through the gate and on out to them islands."

"Where do you store the Purple Pirate costume, Captain?"

"Out there on the islands. We keep all the costumes in a shed out there. It's more efficient."

"Is the shed locked?"

"No, I'm afraid not."

"So anyone who knew the costume was there could have used it."

"I suppose so, Jupiter," Captain Joy agreed.

"Which doesn't help us much," Jupiter said, sighing unhappily. Then he brightened. "But we know now where Karnes is digging, and the real question is, What is he looking for? It must be something hidden in the tower, Mr. Evans, or the tunnel itself."

Joshua Evans shrugged. "I haven't the foggiest idea what it could be."

"Captain?" Jupiter asked.

"I suppose it has to be something left behind by the Purple Pirate, even though the place was torn apart pretty well when people dug all around the cove a hundred years ago."

"Something left by the Purple Pirate is most likely," said Jupiter, "although there was smuggling and other criminal activity at the cove later."

Bob said, "Whatever it is, Jupe, I hope it's still there. I mean, we don't know when they dug through that blocked part."

"We know they were still digging last night," Jupiter pointed out. "Second, go and see if the stakeout is still on."

Pete nodded and trotted toward the front gates. Joshua Evans watched the Second Investigator go with a puzzled look.

"Stakeout?" Evans said. "What stakeout, boys?"

"Karnes has some of his men outside watching the Purple Pirate Lair all day," Bob explained. "Sometimes it's one of them, sometimes two, but someone's always out there."

Evans rubbed his jaw. "All the time, eh?"

"It's one aspect of the case that has me quite puzzled," Jupiter admitted. "It's almost as if Karnes were afraid that someone would take whatever he's after before he can get to it. Or else he knows others are after the same thing he is."

"Maybe whoever was in that Purple Pirate costume," Bob suggested.

Pete came back. "The ice cream wagon is out there, First."

"And you're supposed to go to the taping session again tonight, Captain Joy?" Jupiter asked.

"We sure are," Jeremy answered for his father.

"Then," Jupiter said, his voice firm and determined, "I suggest we all go home and get some rest. We may have a very long night ahead."

He turned to Joshua Evans and Salty Sam. "And I think it would be a good idea for Mr. Evans and Sam to be with us tonight—in case things become more dangerous than we can handle!"

18

A Nasty Shock

Jupiter, Pete, and Bob arrived back at the Purple Pirate Lair on their bikes, carrying their walkie-talkies and flashlights, just as the last tourists were leaving. The Three Investigators were all wearing dark shirts. They slipped in among the exiting tourists to avoid being noticed by Carl in the tree truck, who was now on the stakeout for Major Karnes. Once inside, they hurried to the trailer. The boys shared the Joys' dinner—they all had hearty appetites after the day's adventures.

An hour later Sam Davis joined them. Mr. Evans remained in his tower, showing himself at windows from time to time so that Carl in his cherrypicker would think that all was the same as usual. When it was almost dark, Captain Joy and Jeremy locked the gates and left in their van for the taping session in Rocky Beach.

"Time, fellows," Jupiter said quietly.

They all slipped out of the trailer, keeping to the shadows. If Karnes and his men acted as they had last night, the boys and Salty Sam had about ten minutes to get to the boathouse, and they knew that Carl could be watching their every move. But their dark shirts let them reach the old boathouse without much risk of being spotted.

Inside, Bob and Pete and Sam Davis climbed a steep ladder up into the sail loft while Jupiter plopped into the water and waded under the pier. After opening the drawbridge and locking it behind him, the First Investigator hurried through the tunnel and pressed the lever on the wall. He opened the secret door to the tunnel, closed it behind him, and scurried through the cellar of the stone tower to join Joshua Evans.

In the sail loft Pete and Bob lay in the shadows directly above where the double doors would open and the van drive in if Karnes showed up. Sam took the other end of the loft, where he could watch out the loft window in case anyone came by water. In their positions, they settled down to wait.

Out in the cool June night cars passed from time to time on the cove road. A dog barked in the village across the water. Someone sang somewhere. One of the air taxis took off with a momentary flash of light through the front window of the sail loft. A van door closed! A low squeal of brakes sounded.

A squeal of brakes that seemed to come from the front gates! The sharp click of metal against metal in the near distance. The low purr of a smooth almost muffled engine that came closer in the night. Then a silence.

The double doors opened!

Pete and Bob held their breath. Then they heard the soft engine purr into the boathouse and looked straight down on the top of the van as it drove in. Major Karnes and Hubert jumped out to close the boathouse doors. Bob breathed three times into his walkie-talkie, the boys' prearranged signal.

A faint tap came over Bob's instrument, the return signal from Jupiter.

As soon as the boathouse doors were closed, the little major and Hubert hurried to the side of the pier and jumped into the shallow water. Their flashlights probing the darkness under the pier, they waded to the tunnel entrance and . . .

A loud clatter echoed through the empty

boathouse like a sudden artillery barrage!

"Jumpin' Jehoshaphat!" Salty Sam cried.

As Pete and Bob watched, horrified, the clumsy handyman sprawled on the floor of the sail loft in a tangle of old boards and rope as if he had tripped over something while making some move. Before they could go to his aid or hide themselves, a large mast somehow dislodged by Sam's fall crashed down on them. Then the beam of a flashlight shone directly into the boys' faces.

"All right, you two, get down from there!"

By the door of the van, Carl stood glaring at them—with a flashlight in one hand and a pistol in the other. Gulping, Bob and Pete climbed slowly down the steep ladder. The major and Hubert had climbed back up onto the pier and stood dripping water behind Carl.

"Look up in that loft," the major ordered Hubert. "See if anyone else is up there."

The big man nodded and began to climb up the ladder, which groaned beneath his weight. Major Karnes stared at Pete and Bob, his sharp eyes boring into them.

"I've seen you two somewhere before!" He went on staring at them as the massive Hubert stumbled around in the sail loft above. "By thunder, yes! You were the boys who helped me with that angry mob on the first day of the

interviews. The first boys I interviewed! What
the devil are you doing here? And where's the
other one of you? There were three, I remember. A rather plump boy, who did most of the
talking. Where is he, and what were you two
doing hiding in that sail loft?"

"W-we . . . weren't . . ." Bob stammered.

Hubert called down from the loft, "No one
else hiding out up here, boss!"

Bob and Pete looked at each other. Where was
Salty Sam? What was he up to? Clearly, he must
have climbed out the loft window and escaped.

"Look hard, you fool!" Major Karnes called up
to the loft. "There should be a third boy." He
looked back at Bob and Pete. "Now tell me what
you're doing hiding in this boathouse."

"We weren't hiding," Bob said. "We just fell
asleep. I mean, we went on the pirate ship ride,
got tired, and came in here to rest a while and
just fell asleep."

"Sure," Pete agreed quickly. "We fell asleep."

Hubert climbed down the ladder, slipped,
crashed through the last three rungs, and
knocked Pete sprawling.

"You clumsy oaf!" Karnes cried.

Stammering, Hubert bent to help Pete up.
"S-sorry, feller." He brushed apologetically at
the tall Investigator's clothes, then stared at

Pete. "Hey, boss? Remember I told you I maybe seen a kid watchin' us last night when we went out the gates? This is the kid, you know? I mean, I think."

"So!" Karnes said. "Carl, search them both!"

Carl found their flashlights, cards, and walkie-talkies.

Karnes read their cards. "Detectives, eh? So that's it. You spotted us and tailed us, and the other boy is waitin' for you to tell him what we're doing." He grabbed Pete's walkie-talkie unit. "Are you there, boy? Listen carefully. We've got your pals. We're going to tie them up and leave a man with them. Stay out of our way and don't try any tricks, or you won't like what we do to your friends!"

19

The Tables Are Turned

In the living room of the stone tower Jupiter and Mr. Evans heard the whole scene in the boathouse through Jupe's walkie-talkie, left on receive for Bob's next message. They heard Karnes's final grim warning.

"They've caught them," Jupiter said desperately.

"Steady, Jupiter," Mr. Evans warned.

"But we have to do something!"

"I don't know what," Evans admitted. "Perhaps we—"

There was a frantic knocking at the front door. Jupiter froze. Joshua Evans pulled his pistol from his coat pocket. The knocking came again. Insistent. Mr. Evans walked quietly to the door and pulled it open.

Sam Davis stood there, his legs sopping wet. He hurried into the room looking back over his shoulder.

"That major feller, he caught the boys!"

"We know," Evans said. "How did you happen to get away?"

"Was up front in that loft, got out the window," Sam panted. "Had to jump into the dang water and slog my way out."

"You were lucky," Evans said. "And maybe we are too. Now that you're with us, Sam, I'm beginning to see a plan of action."

"What plan, sir?" Jupiter asked.

"We'd better get down to the cellar first."

The three of them hurried down the cellar stairs into the dim light of the low-ceilinged basement. At Evans' request, Sam hid under the stairs. Jupiter and Evans crossed over to the storeroom.

"What we gonna do, Evans?" Sam whispered hoarsely.

Jupiter echoed, "Yes, Mr. Evans, what is your plan?"

"Well, Jupiter," Mr. Evans said, "I'm afraid it starts with a confession. You see, I—"

"You already found the treasure!" Jupiter exclaimed. "You returned to Pirates Cove because you knew it was here!"

"Yes, Jupiter. I did come back just to find the old treasure, and I found it a week ago!"

"You mean it's still in the tower?"

Evans nodded. "Right here in this storage room. Just as I found it, old Chinese chest and all. You see, long ago my father told me about this tower and the treasure my great-great-grandfather had hidden here. It wasn't until last year that I could leave the East and return to the tower. After a lot of searching, I found the treasure just last week."

"But, sir," Jupiter said, "why didn't you tell anyone you'd found it?"

"To tell you the truth, Jupiter, I wasn't sure what my legal position is, who the treasure really belongs to. Until I was sure, I thought it better to keep it all quiet."

"I should think it belongs to anyone who finds it on his property at this late date," Jupiter decided.

Sam said from across the cellar, "Belongs to anyone can get it, I say. Finders, keepers!"

"In any case," Evans said, "I'm going to make sure it doesn't fall into the hands of your Major Karnes or any other thief!"

"How?" Jupiter said.

"By fooling him, I hope—and we don't have much time. I expect he's taking so long because he's tying up the boys and making his own plans. But he'll be here in the cellar soon, he'll be armed, and he won't be alone. He'll expect to see Jupiter but not Sam, so you stay hidden under those stairs, Sam. I'll admit to him that I've found the treasure and that it's in the storeroom. He'll be so eager, he and his cohorts, that he'll take me right into the storeroom to make me show them where it is, and he'll forget all about Jupiter. So the moment we're all in the storeroom, you come out fast, Sam, and you and Jupiter slam the storeroom door and lock it with a padlock on the outside."

As Evans went into the storeroom to find a padlock, Jupiter objected, "But you'll be trapped in there with them!"

"I have my gun," Mr. Evans said, coming out with a large lock and handing it to Sam, "and I think I can guarantee to capture them. They'll be so surprised when the door closes that they'll run to try to open it—people always react that way. I'll get the drop on them, and I'll hold them until you two free Bob and Pete and bring the police."

"Jumpin' catfish," Salty Sam whispered across the cellar, "here they come!"

"Stand a little behind me, Jupiter!" Evans

said. "Sam, if my plan doesn't work, be ready to jump them! All right, here we go."

Evans positioned himself in the center of the main cellar just as the wall began to slide open. When it was fully open, Karnes and Carl strode into the cellar with their pistols in front of them. They saw Joshua Evans and Jupiter immediately.

"So, the third boy detective and Mr. Joshua Evans himself," the little major said with a laugh. "I should have known you'd be behind those junior snoops in the boathouse, Evans. All right, let's stop playing games. Hand over the goods right now!"

Mr. Evans shrugged. "Okay, Karnes, you win. Leave these kids out of it. What you want is in the storeroom in a cabinet on the rear wall."

Carl holstered his gun as he ran toward the storeroom door.

"Carl!" Karnes snapped. The man stopped, and Karnes waved his pistol toward Joshua Evans. "You go first, Evans. Go ahead, move!"

Evans walked into the storeroom with Major Karnes and Carl close behind him. Karnes never took his eyes off Evans' broad back, as if he were sure Evans was going to try to pull some trick. As they vanished into the storeroom Carl pushed ahead in his eagerness to reach the cabinet on the far wall.

Jupiter was totally forgotten, as Evans had predicted. Sam scrambled out from under the stairs. Quickly he and Jupe pushed the heavy storeroom door closed, and Sam snapped the massive old padlock shut!

There was a long moment of silence, and then shouts of rage and the sound of running feet on the other side of the door. The doorknob was turned, rattled, pulled on! Then Joshua Evans' cool voice spoke on the other side.

"I've got you both covered. Put those guns down easy. Nice and easy. Now turn around. Okay, Jupiter, go get the police."

"On our way!" Jupiter cried.

He could hear Joshua Evans chuckle softly inside the storeroom and could almost see him grinning at the furious Major Karnes and Carl.

20

The Criminals Captured

Tied hand and foot, Pete and Bob sat against the van in the dim boathouse. Hubert guarded them like some great, nervous dog. He held a flashlight in his shaky hand.

"You don't give me no trouble, you know? Boss says I got to not let you get away, so don't you try nothing!"

But Hubert was much too nervous to stand over them for long. He padded over to the water and shone his light under the dock as if hoping to see Major Karnes. Then he padded back to warn the boys again not to give him trouble, and went on to the doors of the boathouse to look outside for any danger that might be sneaking up on him.

He was down at the end of the boathouse dock when a soft hissing seemed to come from Bob's jacket pocket.

"Records," Pete whispered. "It's your walkie-talkie. You left it on. Can you reach it to push transmit?"

Bob squirmed as silently as possible and managed to get his bound hands to the outside of his jacket pocket. After a few tries he pressed the right button through the cloth. He spoke aloud.

"You've got us tied up good in this boathouse, Hubert. You don't have to worry about us getting loose."

Then Bob found the receive button through the cloth and pressed it. Jupiter's voice came very low.

"I understand. Listen carefully. Tell Hubert that Karnes wants to talk to him. He knows Karnes has one of our walkie-talkies, so he should come and listen. I'll handle the rest."

Pete called, "Hubert!"

The giant looked up. "You ain't supposed to talk."

"Okay," Bob said, "but Major Karnes told us to tell you he wants to talk to you."

"Talk?" The mammoth man looked around to see where the major was in the boathouse.

"On our walkie-talkie," Pete said. "You know,

those little hand radios? The major took one of ours, remember?"

"Radio? Oh, yeah, I remember. The boss, he's talking on one of them?"

"Sure," Bob said. "Come and listen."

Hubert came slowly toward them, suspicious of a trick but too scared of Karnes to risk not doing what the major said.

Suddenly the walkie-talkie boomed out, "Hubert, you dolt, when I say I want to talk to you, I mean it!"

Bob and Pete would have jumped two feet into the air if they hadn't been tied up. It was an exact duplicate of the major's voice, to the last quirk. No matter how often they had seen and heard Jupiter's skill at acting and mimicking, they were always startled by their friend's amazing ability to duplicate almost any voice. Hubert went pale, staring at Bob's pocket as if it were the major himself.

"Y-y-yes, boss."

"Stop stammering, you idiot! Now listen to me. Make sure those two boys are tied up, take their walkie-talkie away, then come on through the tunnel and join us! And I mean right away, you fool!"

Hubert nodded rapidly to Bob's pocket. "Sure, boss. Right now. I'm coming."

In his anxiety to do what the major said, poor Hubert even forgot to check Bob and Pete's ropes before he clumsily grabbed the radio, scrambled under the pier, and sloshed on into the narrow tunnel entrance. The instant he was gone, the doors of the boathouse opened and Sam Davis scampered in to untie Bob and Pete.

"We got the major and Carl trapped in the back room of the cellar," Sam chuckled. "Evans tricked 'em, and he's got a gun on 'em too. Evans he already found that treasure and he tricked the major right into that storeroom!"

"Mr. Evans has the pirate treasure?" Bob said as he stood up.

"Had it before I even started lookin'," Sam admitted.

Pete untied his feet. "So it *was* you in the Purple Pirate costume! Looking for the treasure and trying to scare us!"

Sam hung his head. "I come back one night cause I fergot somethin', and I saw them guys leave the boathouse. It took me a couple days to find that tunnel. I just wanted to look for whatever they was after. Never meant no harm."

"Never mind that now," Bob urged. "Let's get out of here before Hubert figures it out and comes back!"

They ran across the dark grounds to the stone

tower. Inside, Jupiter was waiting with his walkie-talkie in his hand. As soon as he saw them he bent over the instrument.

"Hubert, you imbecile! Get back to the boat-house! You've been tricked! That wasn't me talking earlier, you idiot! Get your carcass back to the boathouse right now! If they've escaped I'll have your hide! Hurry, you fool!"

They all listened. Far below they thought they heard the sound of a loud whimpering and then a muffled scrambling back toward the boathouse. They all laughed.

"Wow, some impersonation, Jupe!" Pete cried.

"But what do we do now?" Bob asked.

Before Jupiter could answer, they heard the sudden revving of an engine. As they ran outside they saw the van careen out of the boathouse, turn on two wheels into the main promenade, and race toward the front gate. Hubert crashed the van right through the gates and vanished into the night.

"He acts like the devil's after him!" Pete said.

"Just Major Karnes," Jupiter said, "and it's time we turned that particular devil over to the police."

The Three Investigators' old friend Chief Reynolds was working late and heard their story from the officer on desk duty. The chief immediately sent some men to capture the henchman Santos and bring Captain Joy and Jeremy to the Purple Pirate Lair. Chief Reynolds then got in touch with the county sheriff, and they all raced, sirens screaming, to Pirates Cove. By the time they reached the stone tower, Captain Joy and Jeremy and the other policemen had caught up with them.

"We caught the one named Santos," a policeman reported.

"Good," the chief said. "Let's get the others."

In the cellar the police drew their guns as Jupiter unlocked the massive padlock and swung the heavy door open.

"All right," the sheriff said, "come out with your hands up."

A glum-looking Carl and a red-faced Major Karnes marched out of the storeroom with their hands in the air. Smiling, Joshua Evans came out behind them still carrying his pistol. The police promptly clamped handcuffs around the wrists of the criminals.

"Exactly what are you charging us with?" Major Karnes demanded.

"I expect breaking and entering will do," Jupiter said.

"Or possibly attempted burglary, assault, illegal possession of a concealed weapon, and even kidnapping of the boys!" Chief Reynolds added.

Joshua Evans said, "You got them all?"

"All except Hubert," Bob said, laughing. He told Evans about Jupiter's trick on the massive watchdog. "I'll bet he won't stop driving until that van runs out of gas!"

But Jeremy could stand it no longer. "Hey, guys! Mr. Evans! Where's the treasure?"

Mr. Evans grinned. "Come on."

He led them across the storeroom to a large cabinet along the rear wall. Out of the cabinet he took a shiny black lacquered box with glistening brass fittings and the name LT. WILLIAM EVANS burned in the top. He placed the chest on a table and flung open the cover.

"Gosh," Jeremy breathed.

They all gaped at the mounds of rings, pendants, bracelets, gold candlesticks, silverware, and a lot more that shined and glittered even in the dim light. Bob picked up a brooch. Pete and Jeremy plunged their hands into the mass of jewelry. Jupiter picked up a ring, then carefully fingered the beautiful Chinese chest itself.

"It must be worth millions," Bob said.

"You're a fortunate man, Evans," Chief Reynolds said. "I suggest you hire a lawyer to be sure that everything is legal, but I can't see what could go wrong. Even if this was pirate loot, there's no way of proving that now, and it was found on your property. As the piracy was committed when California was part of Mexico, the Mexican government might try to claim the treasure, but there's no way they could possibly succeed."

"I'll certainly take your advice, Chief," Evans agreed.

The sheriff ordered his men to take Carl and Major Karnes to the Rocky Beach jail to join Santos. Chief Reynolds sent his men with them to start the dragnet for Hubert.

"Well, boys," the chief said, smiling, "another fine job of detection. I'm proud of you as always, but now it must be time for you to start home. The least I can do is give you a lift."

"I certainly want to thank the boys," Joshua Evans agreed. "Perhaps they would like to come and help me inventory my find tomorrow, eh? I expect those crooks will be out on bail soon enough, and I want the treasure safe in a bank."

"They won't make bail until tomorrow noon at the earliest," Chief Reynolds said. "I don't expect they'll bother you even then, but to be sure, I'll leave a man on guard at least until Hubert is caught."

"And Dad and I could help you inventory the

treasure right now!" Jeremy cried.

"Well, everyone wants to help," Mr. Evans said. "And I want to reward my three investigators. Boys, take a piece of the treasure each."

Eagerly the Three Investigators crowded around the black lacquered chest. Pete took a large gold and emerald brooch, Bob a diamond bracelet, and Jupiter a sapphire and diamond ring. Then they piled their bikes into the police van and got a ride home.

21
Escape!

At eight o'clock the next morning Pete sat bolt upright in his bed. Someone was scratching on his window. He looked more closely and saw the branch of a tree brushing against it. He laughed and turned over to go back to sleep. Then he jumped out of bed and ran to the window. There wasn't any tree outside his room!

Down in the gray morning light Jupiter and Bob were waving frantically for him to come down. The neighbors' yard would have to wait till later. He dressed hurriedly and tiptoed down the stairs so that his parents, eating breakfast in the kitchen, wouldn't hear him. Outside in the morning fog, Bob and Jupiter were waiting with their bikes.

"What's up, guys?" Pete asked.

"Jupe thinks something's happened to Captain Joy and Jeremy," Bob said as he mounted his bike.

"What's happened to them?" Pete exclaimed.

"Get your bike and come with us. We can talk on the way to Pirates Cove," Jupiter said grimly.

As the Three Investigators pedaled hard up the northbound highway, Jupiter continued, "I don't know what happened to Captain Joy and Jeremy. I tried to call them this morning and there was no answer at the trailer. I tried to call Mr. Evans too, but the tower didn't answer either."

"But isn't there a police guard at the tower?" Pete said.

"Not now. I called Chief Reynolds' office and they told me that Hubert was captured very early this morning a hundred miles north of Rocky Beach. Karnes, Carl, and Santos are still in jail, so they took the guard off the tower."

"But," Pete said, frowning, "who would want to hurt the captain, Jeremy, and Mr. Evans if the whole Karnes gang is in jail?"

"I have a strong suspicion, Second, that the whole Karnes gang is *not* in jail!"

When the boys reached Pirates Cove, they stopped outside the broken gates of the Purple Pirate Lair. The gates had been totally wrecked by Hubert's smash through them the night before.

As they locked their bikes to the gates Jupiter said, "Bob, you check the trailer. Pete and I will go to the tower."

At the stone tower Pete and Jupiter found the door open! Inside there was only silence.

"Mr. Evans?"

"Captain Joy! Jeremy!"

There was no answer. Pete climbed to the upper floors. Jupiter searched the ground floor and the cellar. They found no one, and there was no sign of the treasure chest. Bob ran in the front door with Salty Sam right behind him.

"The captain and Jeremy aren't at the trailer, First! Sam says he hasn't seen them this morning, but their van is still here!"

Sam was full of remorse. "All my fault! If I'd spilled the beans about findin' that tunnel instead of tryin' to grab whatever it was those crooks was after, everythin' would've been dandy."

"Don't blame yourself, Sam," Jupiter said, trying to comfort the handyman. "The question now is, where are they, and what is Mr. Evans doing?"

"Evans?" Sam said. "Why, him I knows about. Saw him drive off not half an hour ago."

"Sam," Jupiter cried. "Was he carrying anything?"

Old Sam shook his head miserably. "I don't know for sure, only saw him in his car. Think I maybe saw a couple of suitcases on the seat with him."

"The treasure!" Jupiter exclaimed. "He'd want to keep it right beside him. He's gone, fellows! We're too late! I only hope we're in time to help Captain Joy and Jeremy. We must find them!"

"Mr. Evans?" Pete said, puzzled. "The treasure? Why would Mr. Evans run off with the treasure, Jupe? It was his anyway."

"I think it was his all along, Second, and that's the problem. That's why Karnes and his gang watched the Purple Pirate Lair around the clock, and why they were trying to get into the tower unseen. Joshua Evans has fooled us all!"

Salty Sam said, "He run so fast he didn't even take his cat. Look at the poor critter tryin' to get through that door."

They looked into the kitchen where Joshua Evans' black cat was pawing and meowing at the door into the well with the ladder to the second floor.

"Why does it want to get in there?" Pete wondered. "No one's upstairs, and a cat can't climb a ladder."

Jupiter narrowed his eyes. "Open that door and let it through, Records."

Bob opened the door. The black cat ran straight to the wall at the rear of the well. It began to meow and claw at the wall, then sniff and rub itself against the stones while looking back at the boys and Sam. It seemed to be asking them to help it through the wall.

"First?" Bob said. "Maybe there's a hidden room in there."

"Look for an iron ring!" Jupiter exclaimed. "And a loose stone with a lever behind it like the one that opens the tunnel!"

Pete found the ring, cleverly made to look like part of an old light fixture that had once been an oil lamp. The stone beneath the lamp came out. The lever behind the stone moved easily and had obviously been oiled recently. The wall in front of the meowing cat opened, and the boys and Sam followed the animal into a small study lined with books and leather furniture. Captain Joy and Jeremy sat on the leather couch with their hands and feet tied and their mouths covered with tape!

"Cap'n!" Sam cried.

"Jeremy!" Bob and Pete called.

"What happened?" Jupiter exclaimed.

"Ummmmmmmmmmmmmmmmmm!" Captain

Joy and Jeremy mumbled, their eyes saying, Cut us loose before asking questions!

Pete got out his pocket knife and cut the ropes while Bob pulled off the tape as gently as he could.

"It was Evans!" Captain Joy cried as he rubbed at his mouth where the tape had been. "I don't know why. He just—"

"He took the treasure!" Jeremy said as he stamped his feet to get the circulation back. "He aimed a gun at us, made me help tie up Dad, and then tied me up!"

"When did all this happen?" Jupiter wanted to know.

"About an hour ago, Jupiter," Captain Joy fumed. "We'd been up all night sorting out the treasure, and we'd just finished when he pulled his gun and tied us up!"

"Captain Joy, did he say where he was going?"

The captain shook his head. "No, and what I don't —"

"Dad? He made that telephone call," Jeremy said.

"But we didn't hear what he said, son," Captain Joy declared. "I just don't understand it. The treasure was all his."

"Think, Captain! Anything he said on the telephone."

Captain Joy shook his head again. "I told you. We heard nothing. We'd been tied up, and all I was thinking about was why. We'd finished helping Evans sort the treasure. Jeremy did tell Evans that some of the treasure seemed a little funny to him, but . . ."

"What seemed funny, Jeremy?" Jupiter asked.

"I don't know for sure, Jupe," Jeremy said, frowning. "I mean, some of the rings and things looked too . . . too . . . *new.*"

"Yes," Jupiter said. "That's—"

"First!" Bob suddenly cried.

The Records and Research man of the team was standing at the study desk looking down at the notepad beside the telephone book. Jupiter and the others went to the desk. On the notepad there was a crude drawing, a doodle of the sort made unconsciously while talking on the telephone. The drawing of a bird, or an airplane, or . . .

"It's a seaplane!" Jeremy realized. "See the pontoons for landing on water!"

Captain Joy said, "It looks like one of the air taxis over in the Pirates Cove village."

"The air taxi service!" Pete and Bob cried.

Jupiter was already running out of the study toward the outside door.

"Wait!" Captain Joy called. He looked at his

watch. "It's eight forty-five, boys. The taxi office opens at eight-thirty. We'd never get there in time to stop him even if he hasn't gone off already."

"Call the taxi office," Jupiter said. "Maybe we can prevent Evans from taking off! Tell them he's a dangerous criminal!"

Captain Joy looked up the seaplane service in the telephone book, then dialed the number. He told the man who answered that a dangerous criminal was escaping in one of their planes, and he described Joshua Evans. The man said yes, Evans was there. In fact, he was already aboard the air taxi, ready to leave.

"Try to stop him!" Captain Joy said urgently. "Use your radio, tell the pilot anything to get him back!" The captain waited. "What? You can't?" The captain looked back at the boys and Sam. "There's no answer from the air taxi plane! They think Evans has a gun and won't let the pilot answer! They're calling the sheriff, but the plane's already leaving the dock!"

Jupiter and the others ran outside and stood on the shore of the cove looking across to the air taxi dock in the distance. They could see the small seaplane moving slowly away from the dock.

"Too late!" Jupiter said in despair. "We can't stop him now."

Captain Joy joined them at the edge of the cove. He looked at the distant seaplane and then started to run.

"Yes, we can! Come on!"

And the captain ran straight toward the *Black Vulture*!

22
Attack of the Black Vulture

Captain Joy stood at the wheel of the *Black
Vulture*, his eyes bright, as the pirate ship
plunged out across Pirates Cove. A wind was
blowing the thin fog away. Salty Sam had scrambled up to the foremast crow's nest, where he
shouted down instructions to the captain. The
Three Investigators and Jeremy stood in the bow
of the ship as it plowed through the water of the
cove on its first real attack!

"Which way will the air taxi take off?" Jupiter
asked anxiously.

"Straight down the main channel, toward the
ocean," Jeremy said, pointing. "Between those red
buoys and those black buoys. It has to use that

path to face into the wind coming in from the sea."

Up in the crow's nest Sam Davis yelled down, "He's left the dock, Cap'n, and he's pickin' up some speed toward the channel!"

In the bow the boys gauged distance and angles as they stared toward the far-off seaplane.

"We won't make it!" Pete wailed. "It'll get off before we can block the channel!"

"I think we *will* make it!" Bob cried. "It hasn't even reached its takeoff point yet!"

Pete eyed the distance. "Going to be pretty close."

"If we don't get near enough," Jupiter groaned, "it could take off right over us."

"Not with our masts," Jeremy pointed out. "All we have to do is cross the channel in time."

Going at full speed, with all its flags streaming and its banners whipping in the wind, its bow slicing white water and its motor shaking the whole ship, the *Black Vulture* charged toward the middle of the cove.

The air taxi had moved now to the head of the long line of channel buoys. It sat motionless in the water. As the boys watched from the bow of the plunging *Black Vulture*, and Salty Sam peered from the crow's nest, the single propeller

of the seaplane began to whirl faster and faster as
its motor revved up. The plane began to shake in
the water, the speed of its engine going higher
and higher. Then, slowly, it started to move!

Gathering speed, the frail craft began to race
down the channel on its slim pontoons.

Jupiter shaded his eyes. "I can see the pilot
and the passenger! It *is* Evans, and . . ."

The seaplane grew larger every second!

"That red buoy is the halfway mark for takeoff!" Jeremy shouted.

The air taxi passed the red buoy just as the
prow of the *Black Vulture* surged into the channel.

Everyone on the ship held his breath.

In the plane the white face of the pilot was
open-mouthed. Joshua Evans leaned out his window. He held a gun aimed straight at the *Black
Vulture* as the ship moved across the channel.

"Down!" Captain Joy shouted.

The gun fired once, twice.

For an instant time seemed suspended as the
pistol popped in the wind, the *Black Vulture*
moved directly into the path of the charging
seaplane, and the two racing antagonists con-
verged toward what seemed an inevitable colli-
sion!

Then the seaplane veered sharply, wobbled

out of the channel, tore a wing off on a black buoy, and fell over on its side into the water of the cove.

The *Black Vulture* turned sharply toward the wrecked seaplane. From the ship they could see only the pilot swimming clear of the half-submerged air taxi. When they reached him, Jeremy threw him a life preserver with a rope attached. As they hauled the pilot aboard they suddenly saw Joshua Evans. He was swimming away in the opposite direction, pushing a pair of life preservers with the black lacquered treasure chest on top of them!

"Wow," the pilot said as he flopped dripping onto the deck, "you guys saved my life! That nut had a gun, wouldn't let me turn back or use the radio after the office called me back to the dock. What is he, a bank robber or something?"

"Something very much like that," Jupiter said as the *Black Vulture* set out after the escaping Joshua Evans.

The owner of the stone tower was still trying to swim away with the treasure chest on the two life preservers. But the weight of the chest was too much—it kept tilting and sinking as Evans struggled with it. His dark eyes glared up defiantly at all the faces that lined the rail of the *Black Vulture*. Finally Evans realized he couldn't save both the treasure and himself. He abandoned the chest and began to swim as fast as he could toward the nearest point of land. The chest wobbled and tilted on its life preservers, threatening to sink to the bottom any instant.

"Pete! Bob!" Jupiter cried. "Get the treasure!"

Pete and Bob leaped into the water and grabbed the wobbling chest. Together they swam it to the ship, and Jeremy lowered a rope from the yardarm hoist. Pete and Bob tied the chest in a cradle of rope, and Jeremy activated the motorized hoist and lifted the chest, swung it on board, and lowered it to the deck.

"Now for Evans," Captain Joy said as Pete and Bob scrambled back on board.

The *Black Vulture* resumed full speed and quickly turned directly into the path of the madly swimming Joshua Evans. Sam cried from the crow's nest, "I'll drop a lasso, Cap'n. You fellers jump in and get it around that crook!"

The two Joys plunged into the cove along with Pete and Bob and soon surrounded Evans. Jupiter shouted encouragement from the deck. While the captain and Pete grappled with Evans and held him, Bob and Jeremy slipped the loop of rope over his head and under his arms. In the next instant Salty Sam started the hoist. Evans was snatched high into the air, swung in over the deck, and left dangling high on the yardarm like a trussed chicken, flailing and kicking and swearing at everyone.

"I'll get all of you for this!"

He squirmed and twisted where he dangled, shouting threats down at them all. The captain and the boys climbed back on deck, dripping but triumphant. Captain Joy returned to the wheel and headed the *Black Vulture* back to the Purple Pirate Lair.

"All right, Jupiter," the captain said as he steered toward his own dock, "you'd better tell us what this is all about, and just who Evans really is."

"My guess, sir, is that he's some kind of professional thief," Jupiter said grimly. "And he's a fifth member of Major Karnes's gang!"

"Gosh, Jupe, how do you figure that?" Jeremy wondered.

"Primarily, Jeremy, because the 'old treasure' isn't a pirate treasure at all. My guess is it's loot from a lot of burglaries, and very modern loot at that!"

High on the yardarm the dangling Joshua Evans cried down to them, "That fat kid is crazy! I'll sue you for this, Joy! Get me down from here!"

"You had better be sure, Jupiter," Captain Joy said.

"I'm quite sure, Captain," Jupiter said firmly. "All along, the one part of the case we couldn't figure out was the around-the-clock stakeout by the gang. I couldn't see any reason that had anything to do with getting you and Jeremy away from the Purple Pirate Lair, so it had to be something else. There had to be more to the case than we knew. They had to be watching someone else."

"Evans!" Bob cried. "They were watching Evans."

"Exactly, Records." Jupiter nodded. "But I admit that it wasn't until Evans showed us the treasure itself that I realized the truth."

"How, First?" Pete cried.

"Yes, Jupiter, how did seeing the treasure help?" Captain Joy wanted to know.

Dangling from the rigging, Joshua Evans flailed and squirmed and swore down at the leader of the detective trio. Captain Joy steered the *Black Vulture* slowly into its berth at the Purple Pirate Lair.

"Quite simple," Jupiter said. "When Evans showed us his treasure in its black Chinese chest, I knew at once that something was wrong. It was the chest! The brass fittings were much too shiny, and the chest itself looked much too light. Today we coat brass to keep it from tarnishing, but in the old days they couldn't do that, so old brass is either tarnished green or black, or it has a much duller shine from being polished. I examined the chest and saw that the brass *was* coated. It was modern brass, and the chest itself was nothing but lacquered plywood! In the middle of the nineteenth century plywood hadn't been invented. It was a modern chest, and someone had recently burned in William Evans' name to fool us!"

"It could have been an old treasure put into a new chest," Captain Joy considered.

"Not if Evans had just found it," Jupiter pointed out. "But to be sure, when Evans gave us a piece of the treasure, I took a ring that looked modern. Early this morning I took it to Mr. Gandolfi, the jeweler. He was quite angry at me for coming to his house before eight o'clock, but he finally told me that the ring had been made less than five years ago! The whole treasure was modern. Evans must have brought it to the tower himself, and he must have known it was all modern. And since Karnes clearly knew Evans had a treasure, it was a good bet that he knew it was modern too, not pirate treasure!"

"But," Bob objected, "if they knew it wasn't pirate treasure, why—"

"Yes, Records," Jupiter said, nodding, "why would they let the police take them to jail *without telling anyone it wasn't pirate treasure?* Why let Evans get away with telling us it *was* pirate treasure? There could be only one answer —it was all stolen loot! Loot that Major Karnes and his gang would lose if they told the truth. And that was when I saw the whole answer."

In the rigging Joshua Evans thrashed and clawed at the rope that held him. "Don't listen to that fat oaf! He knows nothing! I'll put him and all of you in jail!"

"What answer, Jupe?" Jeremy urged.

"That Karnes and his gang couldn't reveal that the treasure was really stolen loot because *they* had stolen it in the first place! Evans knew that—because he was one of the gang too! They were all members of the same gang. Evans had run away with all the loot, and Karnes and the others had come after him to get it back!"

Chief Reynolds' voice boomed out from behind them all, "Exactly right, Jupiter! You've done it again!"

The chief, the sheriff, and four of their men stood on the dock looking up at the *Black Vulture* and Joshua Evans dangling high on the yardarm.

"They're crazy, Chief!" Evans cried, flailing helplessly. "Arrest them! They don't know what they're talking about!"

"I did come to make an arrest," the chief said sternly, looking up at Joshua Evans, "but it won't be these boys. Thanks to them, and to Captain Joy and his quick action, we're not too late. Yes, Jupiter, Major Karnes and his gang are well-known jewel thieves from the East, wanted in at least six states. The whole gang vanished over a year ago, and everyone was afraid they had all escaped with their loot."

"You sent their fingerprints to Washington," Jupiter guessed.

The chief nodded. "A routine procedure nowadays. Their fingerprints matched the gang's, except that all reports said that there were five members of the gang—not four! I have no doubt at all that Evans' fingerprints will prove him to be that fifth member of the band of thieves! Take him away!"

Convulsed with laughter, Sam Davis lowered Joshua Evans into the waiting hands of the police. The struggling descendant of the Purple Pirate was taken away to a waiting police car while Chief Reynolds and the sheriff congratulated the beaming trio of Investigators.

23

Mr. Sebastian Finds a Legacy

Some days later, on another June morning of low fog, the Three Investigators biked up the coast past Malibu and turned off the Pacific Coast Highway onto Cypress Canyon Road. The local road snaked, narrow and dusty, up one of the dry canyons in the foothills of the coast range.

After some distance and seeing no sign of life, the boys reached a ramshackle old building on the left. Formally a restaurant called Charlie's Place, it was now being renovated into a private home. On the side of the building, where there would be a clear view of the sea once the fog lifted, a concrete terrace was being poured. Somewhere inside the building a high voice was singing in oddly accented English.

"Oh I love to be a Happy Farmer hot dog,
A Happy Farmer hot dog is for me,
'Cause when I am a Happy Farmer hot dog,
Everyone will want to swallow me!"

As the cheerful but broken singing went on, a thin man with graying hair and a somewhat sad face limped out of the building with his hands over his ears. He peered at the boys through his glasses, then smiled.

"Well, Jupiter, Pete, and Bob! How nice. Ah, I know, another case for me to introduce, is it?"

"Yes, sir," Jupiter admitted with a grin.

"A pretty tricky one too, Mr. Sebastian," Pete exclaimed.

Mr. Hector Sebastian had once been a private detective back East, but a severe injury had left him with a permanent limp and forced him to retire. He had turned his knowledge and talents to the writing of suspenseful books and chilling movies. Now rich and growing famous, he had met the boys on a recent case and they had soon become good friends. Mr. Sebastian was always ready to help the team with a little professional advice and enjoyed being involved even from a distance in the boys' investigations. The mystery writer had agreed to try to fill the large shoes of their former mentor, the late Mr. Alfred Hitchcock, and introduce their cases.

But at the moment Mr. Sebastian was looking at the boys with a bemused expression. "I would never have expected cowardice in you boys."

"Cowardice, sir?" Pete wondered.

"What else can I call your failure to telephone me to say that you were coming? Obviously you did not have the courage to announce yourselves and face the music of what Don would whip up for you out of the latest *TV Guide!*"

The boys laughed at this reference to the packaged concoctions featured in television commercials and so exuberantly prepared by Mr. Sebastian's Vietnamese houseman, cook, and general assistant, Hoang Van Don.

"But don't think you're home free," Mr. Sebastian warned. "I assure you that Don can produce an even more inedible dish in five minutes, which he will do the instant he sees you. As a matter of fact, that could be a blessing. Anything he cooks must be better than the jingles he sings, so come in and I shall read your report while Don prepares another delight."

They followed Mr. Sebastian up onto the rickety wooden porch, then in through a lobby that now smelled like the hot dog stand at Dodger Stadium in Los Angeles. Beyond the lobby was a mammoth room that had once been the dining room of Charlie's Place. The floors were polished hardwood, and huge plate-glass windows opened out over trees and a vast view of the foggy ocean. At the moment sliding glass doors were being installed between the enormous room and the new terrace. The room itself was almost bare of furniture, but there was a low glass-topped table and some patio chairs around a big stone fireplace at one end. At the other end of the room, partially hidden by tall bookshelves, sat a big desk and a typewriter table.

"The writing has been going better since I've started introducing your cases," Mr. Sebastian said. "You seem to help my mental processes. I'm anxious to read your report. But first you must brave Don's tender mercies!"

He called to his houseman. The terrible singing ceased, and a smiling Oriental man appeared in the lobby. Not much taller than Jupiter, and very slim, Hoang Van Don grinned broadly when he saw the boys. He plainly liked them. He hurried forward, then stopped, horrified.

"Ah, have nothing for lunch! First you eat! Have all-meat Happy Farmer hot dogs, brought fresh from East, for Mr. Sebastian dinner casserole, recipe on package. But can cook more. Make quick one-hundred-percent imitation artificial Bora-Bora punch of nine fruit-flavor juices. Also two-minute homemade cake ready with no cooking!"

"We can hardly wait," Mr. Sebastian sighed, as Hoang Van Don left happily. "I long for the gourmet meals of the lowest fast-food chain. But never mind my misadventures at the dining table. What is our case today?"

"We call it the Mystery of the Purple Pirate!" Bob said as he took a large envelope out of his backpack and handed it to Mr. Sebastian.

Don reappeared almost instantly with the hot dogs, genuine imitation artificial fruit punch, and two-minute homemade cake. Oblivious to Mr. Sebastian's bleak looks at the food, the boys ate happily while the writer returned to reading the report.

"An interesting case," he said when he had finished. "A severe test of detective skills and equipment, as well as your powers of observation and reasoning. I assume that this Joshua Evans did turn out to be a member of the Karnes gang?"

"Yes, sir," Jupiter said, nodding. "His fingerprints were on file in Washington. Once Evans was in jail, Karnes knew the game was up and he told the whole story. They had been stealing for years. The gang had gathered all that loot, and then Evans stole it and disappeared."

"And they are all now in jail, with heavy charges against them?"

"You bet," Pete exclaimed. "Six states in the East are fighting over who gets first shot at them!"

"It's not always good to be popular," Mr. Sebastian said dryly. "I take it Karnes invented his entire pirate-interview operation just to get Captain Joy and Jeremy away?"

"Yes, sir," Jupiter said. "There isn't any such organization as the Society for Justice to Buccaneers, Brigands, Bandits, and Bushwhackers."

"In a way that's too bad," Mr. Sebastian sighed. "It had a fine ring to it! And the around-the-clock stakeout was to make sure Evans didn't run off with the loot again before the gang could get into the tower and find it?"

"Sure," Bob said. "And Evans tied up Captain Joy and Jeremy because he was afraid they would guess the truth after Jeremy commented on how new some of the jewelry looked."

"Only Jeremy never thought anything more of it," Pete said. "He wasn't suspicious at all!"

"The error of a guilty man," Mr. Sebastian said. "And a desperate one. He must have cooked up his scheme to fool everyone on the spur of the moment."

"He did," Jupiter nodded. "We gave him the idea by talking about pirate treasure. When he realized Karnes and the gang had found him and he couldn't get away with the loot without being caught by them, he decided to use us all against each other. He had plenty of time to burn William Evans' name in the chest and put it into the storeroom, and he had various alternative plans."

Mr. Sebastian nodded. "It takes great intelligence to size up a situation and take advantage of circumstances. Too bad he used his intelligence for criminal purposes."

"Captain Joy is a fast thinker too. He was smart to use the *Black Vulture* to stop the air taxi," Bob said. "And he got an unexpected bonus—a lot of insurance companies had offered rewards for the return of that loot! Captain Joy offered to share the money with us, but we told him to use it to make the Purple Pirate Lair a super show."

"Something it badly needs, judging by your report," Mr. Sebastian agreed.

"But the captain was swell enough to give us the money for a new trailing device," said Pete. "And he adopted Blackbeard, Evans' homeless cat. Said it would add atmosphere to the Lair."

"What about that document Karnes and his crew were studying," Mr. Sebastian asked. "Was it a map?"

"Yes, but just a map of Pirates Cove," Bob explained. "The major had no map that showed where the tunnel was."

"But you said in the report it was impossible to

find the tunnel unless you knew it was there. How did Karnes find it?"

Jupiter laughed. "Evans himself told Karnes about the tower and the tunnel one time years ago when they were hiding from the police. Except Karnes didn't know where the tower was and Evans didn't know the tunnel's location. Evans' father had told him the tunnel had collapsed and was useless, so Evans thought it not worth looking for. Evans returned to the tower with the stolen jewels, and it took the rest of the gang a full year to track him down. In searching the tower grounds for the treasure, Karnes discovered the tunnel's boathouse entrance. He and Hubert dug it out so they could sneak into the tower and search for the treasure there."

"And what happened between Evans and Karnes inside that storeroom?"

Bob said, "Evans simply reminded Karnes that if he denounced Evans to the police, none of them would ever keep the loot. Karnes didn't have much choice—tell and lose it all; keep quiet and let Evans get away. I guess Karnes figured he had a better chance of getting the loot eventually by going along with Evans."

"So in the end there was no pirate treasure at the Purple Pirate Lair," Mr. Sebastian said, "but perhaps a legacy from the Purple Pirate."

"A legacy, sir?" Jupiter asked.

"From the Purple Pirate, Lieutenant William Evans, to his great-great-grandson, Joshua Evans! A legacy of piracy and other thieving crimes! In the end, Joshua Evans proved to be every bit as much a pirate as his notorious ancestor!"

The Three Investigators

Mystery Series

THE THREE INVESTIGATORS
C R I M E B U S T E R S™